DEATH BEFORE DINNER

or

Professor Axton Beauséjour and the Case of the Nuptial Demise

by Rachele Alson

Dedicated to those special twenty who brought the story to life originally

Published by Tribeca Studios in Australia.
Copyright © Rachele Alson 2025
Rachele Alson has asserted her right to be identified as the author of this work.

Professor Beauséjour created by Ryan Alcock.
Luna Rochique and Dana Spectra created by Ryan Alcock and used with kind permission.

Cover art by Ryan Alcock.
First published in 2025.

A catalogue record for this book is available from the National Library of Australia

Contents

THE ROYAL ARMS

Rest Rooms

Antechamber
(Lauren's
Change Room)

Private Rest
Room

Foyer

Main Hall

Rest Rooms

Kitchen

Antechamber
(Beausejour's
Study)

DRAMATIS PERSONAE

Zakaria Barrera, chef executif to the royal family, and guest

Axton Edevane Sam Beauséjour, former law lecturer to Prince Michael and Luna Rochique, and guest at the wedding

Abel Beddows, butler to Prince Michael

Amy Birman, maid to Princess Lauren

Solomon Burton, chief of royal security and personal bodyguard to Prince Michael, and guest

Lady Jacinta Daniels, wedding guest and cousin of Prince Michael

Dani Kelinaw, Crovanian police inspector

Dr Fabian Kilman, personal physician to Prince Michael, and guest

Lauren, Princess of Crovania, formerly Lauren Foster, the bride

Kendal Leigh, wedding guest and bridesmaid

Dione Lora, the chief bridesmaid and old friend of Princess Lauren

Lucas, Crown Prince of Crovania and younger brother of Prince Michael

Michael, Crown Prince of Crovania, recently married to the victim

Jindra Péťa, wedding guest

Lord Pero Petar, the best man, and childhood friend to Prince Michael

Cameron Regan, wedding guest and business rival to Prince Michael

Blake Reese, godmother to Princess Lauren and guest

Clayton Reese, an old friend of Princess Lauren's father, godfather to the bride, and guest

Luna Rochique, pop sensation and actress, old friend of Princess Lauren and wedding guest

Hunter Shelby, wedding guest and groomsman

Stephanie, Crown Princess of Crovania and sister of Prince Michael

Borna Vanja, wedding guest

Countess Emília Vladan, aunt to Prince Michael and guest

Count Aleš Vladan, uncle to Prince Michael, and husband of Countess Emília and guest

PART ONE

THE TRUTH

Chapter One

Looking Back to Dreamier Times

Club Stars, Scullin

Ten years ago

Club Stars was electric. The crowd moved in time to the music as the beat throbbed in the air. The smell of alcohol and sweat was pungent, but at the same time sweet, and it hung in the air, melting into an aroma that quickly became a drug that was ingested without even knowing it. There was an atmosphere, created from the smells, sounds and lights, mixed together such that if you stepped into the room, it was like touching an electric socket. It was tangible.

Luna Rochique was drunk (and maybe a little bit high), but she could feel the atmosphere reaching forward to touch her, to wrap its arms around her and embrace her. It wanted to kiss her and make love to her, and Luna wanted to do the same in return because it was what she lived for. She snuck a quick glance to the side to see that her backup singers – wittily calling themselves the Heavenly Bodies – were actually making out. She should probably be angry, but it didn't matter. Luna was the star – her voice was what people were cramming into the dark room to hear.

> *When she walks into the room*
> *The sound of heels marking out time*
> *You're nothing except her next meal*
> *But you know she's worth the fine.*
>
> *Succubus to steal your heart*
> *Succubus with eyes like coal*
> *Succubus to break your spirit*

Succubus will steal your soul.

The crowd roared the chorus and Lauren and...what was her name? Luna wanted to say Carly, but she wasn't really sure. She hadn't paid enough attention at the beginning of the night when Lauren had introduced them. Lauren and Carly broke their lip lock to deliver the harmonies as Luna belted out *Kiss from a Succubus*. The band were playing like they'd been the ones to confront the Devil in Georgia, and Luna felt what was almost like an orgasm as the music and crowd performed with her.

They knew her song! They were actual fans!!

Luna and her band played for forty minutes straight, and the crowd didn't want them to stop. At one point they covered an eighties classic, turning it into a wound for the time, digging into it and delivering the pain that the song had. Someone in the crowd genuinely cried (though they were probably just completely off their face, but it was emotion, so take the win).

The set finished, the group staggered off stage into what the owner of Club Stars had called the Green Room (though it looked like some small kitchen that had maybe been converted, without actually moving anything like the fridge, sink or kitchen table out of the space), Lauren grabbed Luna's hand and leaned forward to whisper in her ear, trying to be heard over the explosion of sound emanating from the door to the stage as it remained open behind them.

"We're the bomb, babe!" she bellowed and Luna couldn't help but leave the silly grin on her face that had settled there about thirty minutes earlier. The satisfaction of this success was more than she could have ever hoped for, or dreamed of. Suddenly all the frowns and tuts from her father were being washed away by what was genuine success.

Luna could see the future. She would make it huge, in ways that people would be astonished by. When she was doing a concert, the tickets would sell out in a heartbeat, and then some other people would be flogging them at the front of the venue for ludicrous prices. But Luna would find this out and she would go down and buy all the tickets and then sell them for a reasonable price back through the venue's front office, because she would never let her fans down. Ever.

When people walked up to the venue (and she'd be playing in stadiums – Ron Laver Arena, Allphones Arena, Meninga Stadium), they'd see massive posters with her standing on them, dressed in something fashionable, but also cool, but also very unique to her. They'd pause to take pictures, but then have to move on quickly because there were so many people approaching the stadium that they couldn't afford to waste time for fear of clogging up the avenue.

There would be security, lots of it. What would she have to ban from the concert? Surely, she'd have to ban something. Everyone did that.

Suddenly filled with excitement, she turned to Lauren and kissed the other girl, who in turn kissed her back, both carried away by alcohol, marijuana and adrenaline. It was a heady mix and the bloke-ish cheers around them didn't crush the atmosphere as it would under normal circumstances. Instead, Luna wrapped her arm around Lauren's waist and raised her free hand, clenching her fist.

"We're the fucking bomb!!!!" she bellowed and there were more cheers. Lauren's friend had materialized at Luna's free side, and the singer pulled her in, thinking of nothing more than doing something stupid and exciting.

Something that a real superstar would do.

This was the definite first night of the rest of her life, and Luna was determined to mark it with something she could look back on and say, with false regret, "and that was how I started it all. Probably not the cleverest thing I could have done, but I was only eighteen."

"We're going to be so famous and rich," Luna grinned at Lauren.

"Babe, we are. And we'll be friends forever," Lauren grinned back.

"Primary school, high school and now rock stars!!!" Luna said, unaware that she was screaming at her friend. "We'll never be apart!"

"You'll be at my wedding!!!" Lauren shouted, and at that point someone showered them in something that was probably champagne, but was exactly what was needed to ignite the perfect harmony of teenage success.

Chapter Two

The Chance Encounter of a Lifetime

I

Fabric Club, London

Two years ago

Prince Michael of Crovania felt distinctly uncomfortable and out of place. The youth of London, dressed in clothes that were no match for the weather outside, but were clearly put on to emphasize other aspects of the body, writhed and shook in time to a music that seemed to be nothing more than a dull thud. Once you were approaching forty, these sorts of events held little appeal, and Michael decided he definitely didn't want to be there. And he certainly wouldn't have been if it hadn't been for Hunter Shelby.

He was at that point where he was about to wrap up his degree, and had to admit that despite his initial reservations, and his sister's objections, the decision to come to the UK and get a law degree had turned out to be a good choice. He had been lucky enough to be lectured by one of the most interesting law lecturers he would ever meet, and he had also been lucky enough to make some good friends, including Hunter Shelby. When Lord Pero Petar had told him about the decision to come to England for a surprise visit, Michael had enthused about the visit to Hunter, and Hunter had announced they would have to go out and do something wild. They would get away from Oxford, and they would hit the city.

Hunter had got in contact with one of the students in their course, Dione

Lora, and she had told them about where they should go. The Fabric Club, she had told them, would be the best place ever. It was brilliant. She had a friend who could get them tickets to go in.

And so, Michael stood awkwardly on the balcony surrounding the dance floor inside Fabric – or more accurately, fabric, as it preferred. They had dined at Leicester Square, and met Lauren Foster, and Michael had immediately become smitten. He was at least a decade older than her, if she was the same age as Dione, but he couldn't not be attracted to her. Her long blonde hair shone and her bright blue eyes sparkled. They shook hands, and he noticed the softness of her skin. She had jokingly made comment about his own palms being soft, and asked if he was a Lord. Pero had jokingly replied that he was the lord, and Michael was a Prince. They all laughed, though not actually at the same joke.

But once they had made it to the club (and Lauren had announced they would walk there, because the night air would do them good), Lauren and Dione had merged into the mob as it heaved and throbbed, and Hunter joined them, dancing and grinding. Michael had elected to go to the balcony, Pero with him, the former taking advantage of the fact he didn't have Solomon Burton looming nearby, ever ready to protect him. In the United Kingdom, Michael of Crovania was nothing more than Michael Aspen, which made it very easy to come and go (though the odd photographer was still ever present).

At one point Michael had turned to his best friend to make comment about how they were the oldest people there – and also the most inappropriately dressed, given they were in suits and collared shirts (thank goodness Lauren had made them remove their ties), but was shocked to see that Lord Pero had disappeared. Michael scanned the room, annoyed that his friend had found something – or perhaps someone – more interesting.

It was, he decided, time to go. Time to return to reality and just be himself, rather than trying to fit in with beautiful young things, no matter how interesting he found them. Or how much he hoped they might find him.

And so, he walked out of fabric, out of the double steel doors set into the miserable grey columns lit bright blue, and onto Charterhouse St. There were people milling about, but Michael didn't particularly care. He was going to get a cab and then go back to his hotel.

"Hey," a voice called out, and he ignored it, suspecting it wasn't directed at him.

"Hey, Michael," the voice called again, and this time he turned at his name. And there she was. She was glowing, slightly, her hair a little messy, but her silver dress was in place, highlighting her curves and showing off her legs. She was gorgeous, without doubt. "You're not leaving, are you? Or, to be precise, you're not leaving me, are you?"

"I felt a little like I was," he paused unwilling to finish the sentence.

"Too old?" Lauren asked, and Michael felt the sting a little. "Because you shouldn't," she continued. "You are definitely not too old." She walked up to him, and the people around her seemed to part. "You are whoever you want to be, whenever you want to be. And now, you want to be my boyfriend." Michael didn't know how to deal with that. He wasn't even sure what to say. Normally women would fawn over him because he was a prince, and that was what was expected, but to be…commanded? Ordered? He wasn't sure exactly what was going on, but it was different and exciting.

"I do," he said with a small smile.

"Well, in that case," Lauren said softly, "why don't we do what boyfriends and girlfriends do?"

That first kiss was the one he would never forget.

II

Berdwardshire Castle, Berdwardshire

Six months later

The heir apparent to the throne of Crovania, was rarely nervous, but at the moment, Prince Michael found himself to be definitely in that state. Most things in his life he was completely in control of, and so there was no need to be concerned about anything. Even the relatively small "problem" of needing to be married before ascending to the throne was a detail. Truthfully, the throne would wait. He didn't anticipate a challenge from either of his siblings in that department. After all, it was not like either of them particularly wanted that particular burden.

And yet, if he were honest, he was a little nervous about introducing Lauren to his family. Since returning to Crovania with her, he was uncertain about how people were responding to her. Beddows was standoff-ish, but that was the nature of his personality. He acted that way with everyone, so Michael suspected he was probably just being him.

He had assigned Birman to be Lauren's personal maid. She seemed a little put out by this, and he understood that. He appreciated her loyalty to him, but things had to change and Lauren needed a maid he could trust. So, Birman was that maid.

The rest of the staff all seemed to like her. There was something about a vivacious and exciting, beautiful young woman that had everyone enthralled. Indeed, Birman was doting on her new mistress within a day or so, and Dr Kilman, who had come to give her some inoculations for Crovania seemed particularly taken with her.

However, the staff were the staff. They would like her because it was their job, whether they genuinely felt that way or not. His brother and sister, however, were not so obligated. Nor his aunt or uncle. But while the Count, the Countess and Prince Lucas would be polite in their assessments of his new love, Princess Stephanie would be…well, she would be Stephanie. She held little illusions about life and was more than comfortable in delivering an acerbic opinion, regardless of what the rest of her family thought.

As such, he sat on the couch, in the spacious, but minimalist principal lounge of the castle, Lauren by his side, dressed considerably more demurely than she had been the first night he had met her. There was a polite knock at the door, and it was opened by the stiff figure of Beddows.

"The Count and Countess Vladan, and his royal highness, Prince Lucas," Beddows announced, swinging both doors open so the three could enter. Michael had to admit he was surprised to see Lucas with the older couple, expecting them to arrive separately, and then he wondered if perhaps Lucas had sat in his car waiting for the Count and Countess to arrive.

"Your highness," the Count smiled warmly, hobbling up to him and bowing, before they embraced.

"Uncle Aleš, it's so good to see you," Michael said, as he hugged the old frame warmly. "Aunt Emília," he added, embracing the old lady. She sniffed at his informality.

"Your highness," she finally answered bowing, and all three men laughed at her good naturedly.

"Lucas," Michael smiled, and his younger brother came up and hugged him as well.

"It's good to have you back, Michael," the younger Prince said.

"Do you always call each other by your full names? I'd have thought Mikey and Luke would have been easier," Lauren grinned, and the three newcomers turned to see the stranger.

"Allow me to introduce Lauren Foster," Prince Michael smiled. "My," he paused, before deciding to plunge in. "My new passion. My new love," he said, taking her hand, his face beaming.

"How do you do, my dear," Count Aleš said, holding out a hand, and Lauren took it eagerly.

"My uncle, Count Aleš Vladan, and his wife, Countess Emília."

"I'm so pleased to meet you," Lauren said. The Countess was not quite so engaging, inclining her head pleasantly.

"What a delight" Lucas said, coming forth and shaking her hand. Michael frowned slightly, a little disappointed that his brother was being as hesitant as he was. He had been almost certain that Lucas would have taken to Lauren.

"My younger brother," Michael clarified.

"Oh, you're like a hotter version of your brother," Lauren said, before gripping Michael's arm, playfully. Lucas went bright red.

"Well, you can't have both brains and beauty, I suppose," Michael joked.

"I would argue you could," came a new voice, and the group turned to see the stunning figure of Princess Stepanie at the doorway. She was dressed like an American fashion icon, a slight dress clinging to her figure. She looked like a million dollars, and Michael had no doubt that between the dress and the jewellery, she probably came close. Beddows had an eyebrow raised, but was clearly not going to let his introduction be dismissed.

"Her Royal Highness, Princess Stephanie," he announced.

"I think we all know who I am," Stephanie said dismissively, as she walked down the single stair into the sunken lounge. She walked straight to Lauren, neither woman taking their eyes off the other.

"How do you do?" Lauren asked, hesitantly.

"Oh, I'm wonderful. Yourself?" Stephanie answered, holding out her hand. Lauren took it and lent forward to kiss it, uncertain of what else to do.

"You don't have to do that," Michael said, but Stephanie looked amused.

"Perhaps she understands the importance of first impressions?" Stephanie said, looking at her brother.

"Lunch is served," Beddows announced from the doorway.

"Shall we go?" the Prince asked, and Lauren released Princess Stephanie's hand and nodded.

III

"This looks delightful, Barrera. Honestly, you're a master," Count Aleš said as the entrée was placed before him. They were seated at the extravagant dinner table in the main hall, the gorgeous China plates complemented by the silver cutlery. Three vases were full of lilies (they had been dahlias, but Lauren had revealed she had an allergy to them, and Michael had ordered the flowers to be replaced immediately).

There was no doubting how correct he was. Zakaria Barrera's meal was incredible.

"Sautéed sea scallops with caramelized apples and chicken livers," Barrera announced grandly, his big, black beard bristling with pride.

"Oh, no," Lauren said, her voice sounding devastated. "I'm allergic to sea food."

"Ma'am?" Barrera said, hesitantly. "I thought you enjoyed the coral trout last week."

"Oh, fish is fine. Sea food," she said, and turned to Beddows. "You can take this away. I'll skip the entrée." The look on Beddows face made it clear exactly what he thought of being spoken to like one of the lower staff. It was, however, nothing compared to the look on Barrera's face, though this didn't seem to bother Lauren at all.

"Don't just stand there, Beddows," Lucas said. "Snap to it."

"Of course," Beddows replied, his voice dripping with poison. He moved forward and took the plate, though he handed it to one of the other footmen who took it away.

"Perhaps we might have a salad for Lauren?" Michael said, turning to Barrera. The chef looked as though he were about to say something that might just have resulted in his firing, but instead he bit back his comment and nodded.

"Of course, your highness," he muttered, before heading back to the kitchen. As he left, he seemed to say something else that sounded a bit like "Hopefully you won't find another allergy today," but everyone was sure he wouldn't have said it, so they decided they simply hadn't heard correctly.

"Never mind him, my dear," Count Aleš smiled. "Arty types are always sensitive, aren't they?"

"Lauren is an arty type, Uncle," Michael said. "She's a performer. A singer."

"Can we listen to your music somewhere?" Stephanie purred.

"I always bring a disc with me," Lauren grinned at her.

"Oh, we'll have to retire and listen to it before I go," Stephanie smiled back.

"I do love rock," Prince Lucas enthused, and Michael smiled at how his family were welcoming his new fiancé.

"Sounds like fun," Lauren replied with a grin. Seated opposite each other, only Count Aleš saw Countess Emília's eyebrow raised. "Then you and I, Stephanie, should go shopping. I'm sure Michael wants me to spend his money on amazing clothes." She laughed out loud, seemingly ignorant of the fact she was the only one.

"What do your parents do, my dear?" Count Aleš asked, and Lauren turned to him, her eyes wide.

"Oh, they're dead," she said, and her voice caught slightly in her throat, prompting Michael to reach out to her. "They used to run this business. Uncle Clayton runs it now. Well, he's not really my uncle," she said with a smile. "He's my godfather. But he keeps everything going along nicely."

"Oh, how delightful," the Count murmured.

Countess Emília caught her husband's eye and raised her eyebrow once more.

IV

"I just mean if I knew what you wanted the paperwork for, I could probably get exactly what you needed," Clayton Reese said, and Lauren looked at him.

"I didn't think I'd need to justify asking for my parent's company investments, Uncle Clay," Lauren said, and Clayton laughed, somewhat humourlessly.

"Well, company investments is a broad term, that's all I meant. That could mean a little bit of paperwork, or it could mean a lot, really. Gosh, this is a nice place, here, right? You're going to live here when you marry Mikey?"

"Michael, Uncle Clay, he prefers Michael. Well, you should probably call him your highness, but you know what I mean." Clayton looked as though he had been slapped. "But asking about the Castle isn't going to make me forget what I was talking about." She was standing up, and as she was about to put the glass in her hand down, she seemed to suddenly realise there was nowhere to do it. "Amy!" she called out, and there was a pause before she repeated herself, louder. A little annoyed she turned to look out the window.

The door burst open and her maid came in, somewhat breathless.

"Forgive me madam," she spluttered. Lauren held out her glass, and Amy looked puzzled, not quite understanding what was going on.

"I can't keep holding it forever, Amy," Lauren said, and the maid nodded, taking the glass. "Is Beddows around?" she asked, and Amy widened her eyes.

"You want me to get him?" she asked.

"Now," Lauren said.

"So, until we know exactly what we want, should I just wait for a bit?" Clayton Reese said. Lauren continued to look out the window, whatever having caught her attention clearly holding it with a grip of steel. "Lauren?"

"The last audit," Lauren said, though she was clearly distracted. "Just get me the last audit."

"That's a lot of paperwork," Reese said, his hollow laugh ringing out again. "You can't want it all." Lauren suddenly turned from the window and looked at him.

"I do, Uncle Clay," she said. "I really do. And I want it as soon as possible. Like, tomorrow."

"You're not serious?"

"They have email in Crovania," she replied, silkily.

They stared at each other, Lauren clearly not intending to say anything, Reese clearly struggling to work out what exactly to say. The impasse was broken by the arrival of Beddows, who seemed to have taken to a keeping a permanent look of disdain on his face, presumably so he couldn't be accused of any actual contempt.

"You called, ma'am?" he asked, managing to make it rhyme with "drop dead".

"When did Dione arrive?" Lauren asked and pointed out the window. On the lawn in front of the castle, Prince Michael was strolling and chatting with Dione Lora, who seemed fascinated by everything he was saying, laughing perhaps just a little too much for Lauren's liking.

"I understand she arrived just after Mr Reese did," Beddows said. "We explained that you were with Mr Reese and she offered to spend some time catching up with his Royal Highness."

"Don't do that again," Lauren said. "She's my friend, not his. Bring her straight to me."

"Of course, ma'am," Beddows said archly.

"You got a mouth on you," Reese said, with a chuckle.

"Don't argue with me, Beddows. Do what I say. Without comment." Lauren looked at him, and Beddows opened his mouth to say something, but then clearly thought better of it. He nodded politely to both Lauren and Reese and then turned to leave the room.

"You certainly have that penguin's number," Reese continued to chuckle. It dried up, however, as it became clear that Lauren wasn't interested in what he had to say. "I can't..." he started but she just looked at him. He could tell what it meant. There would be no more words from his goddaughter now. She would ignore him until she had got what she desired.

"Be careful what you wish for, Lauren," he sneered, and stormed out of the room.

PART TWO

THE WHOLE TRUTH

Chapter One

We Are Gathered Here Today

Palace Hotel, Reidon

I

Luna Rochique couldn't remember the last time that she had worn white, and wondered if perhaps it was just a little too on-the-nose. She regarded herself thoughtfully, slightly impressed by the beautiful white satin suit she had opted to wear, with the long slit up the side, showing off an impressive amount of leg (though no doubt the tattoo would be frowned upon). Being of what she would charitably describe as average height, long legs were a luxury that was rarely afforded to her. With the heels and the slit, she actually looked quite leggy for a change, and she couldn't help but feel a little proud. Her shoulder length blue hair had been given a streak of white for the occasion, which her little sister had said was most definitely trying to draw attention away from the bride. It wasn't true, she thought to herself.

Was it?

She felt a twinge of guilt, and told herself again it wasn't true.

Besides, she thought to herself tetchily, if the seating was to be believed she was being placed beside that supermodel, Dana Spectra, and quite frankly she needed something to stand out from the crowd if she was going to be in Dana's shadow.

She suspected that it was a petty act of revenge, to be truthful. But these things were what they were.

Luna went to the window of her room and looked out across the small town of Reidon, which, like she would be with Dana later, was overshadowed by Berdwardshire Castle, just off in the distance. It was to be her destination later today, and she had to admit it looked quite impressive. Three massive wings with turrets and a moat surrounding it, Berdwardshire Castle was definitely the stereotype of a royal home. Luna had some knowledge of castle design (for reasons she was definitely leaving at home on this occasion!), and guessed that the Castle was probably 14th century. A Gothic style with the keep surrounded by the moat, and the pointed arches gave it quite the distinctive look. Ancestral home of the Vladen family, it was to be the new home of the married couple.

Sucking on her lip, she turned and headed out of the room, remembering to close the door and lock it with the key. This was Crovania, not Central London, and the hotels were as old fashioned as the customs; you got a key, not a keycard, and you had to remember to lock your door. It was almost about time to head to the church, she reflected, which meant that the hour was upon them, and before they knew it, Lauren Foster would be Princess Lauren of Crovania.

She stepped out of the quaint little elevator, which had a proper metal gate, complete with charming older gentleman who pulled it open for her to exit. He dipped his hat, and she gave him a warm smile, but wasn't sure that was exactly what he wanted. He didn't make it awkward, and Luna resolved to make sure that she had some cash on her when she left in order to tip the man later.

Crovania, she had discovered after being sent her invite, was a small little autonomous community in Eastern Europe which could be part of several different countries, depending on where the borders fell and who was drawing the map. Almost out of spite, the Crovanians had declared themselves independent from any of the countries which tried to claim it, but was sadly not recognized as such by the UN, much less the US who would have happily handed them over to Russia if it had been necessary. In truth, it was too much hassle for any country to impose authority and so for the most part everyone just nodded and allowed it to happen.

Strangely they never seemed to have a king, rather a prince sat on the throne and was nominally the ruler of the country. The prince could indeed become King, but this had to be unopposed by his family and required the intended recipient to be married. Intriguingly, Crovania hadn't a king for decades, as the siblings of each declarant had opposed the request, meaning that the country's ruler was in flux for a considerable time. Fortunately, the local council essentially governed in their stead.

It was easier that way.

At present, Prince Michael intended to ascend to the throne as King, and for the first time in a while, the intended's siblings seemed content with this situation.

Luna was more than used to travelling around, not only for her concerts, but also for her hobby, and so when the invitation to the wedding came, and her manager cleared her schedule to allow her to attend, she decided it would be worth the trip. The fact she would be in a place where virtually no one knew who she was also appealed. There was nothing quite like anonymity to sell the wedding of a friend from some time ago.

On the street, another staff member of the Palace Hotel, waved a bright yellow taxi down, and Luna had to admit she was surprised at the efficiency of the hotel. The man (who might have been younger than the elevator attendant, but there was a similarity which suggested he was related all the same) held the door open, and Luna stepped forward to get in the car, but was shocked when a man blocked her way.

"Excuse me," snapped the man, before turning to her and softening. He was older than her, probably by about a decade, and was dressed in a dark blue suit with a white necktie. There was something undeniably handsome about him, in a classic Hollywood sort of way, complete with pencil mustache, but there was also a temper behind the eyes. "Sorry," he mumbled, and stepped back, indicating the car.

"Are you going to the wedding?" Luna asked.

"As a matter of fact, yes. Cameron Regan," he said, holding out his hand.

"Luna Rochique," she replied, shaking it. "Perhaps we could go together," she added.

"Well, that's quite kind of you, thank you," Regan replied, and again indicated the car. Luna smiled and got in, followed by Regan.

"I'm a friend of the bride's," she said.

"More than that," Regan responded, and Luna looked at him. "I don't live under a rock, Miss Rochique. I'm aware of your reputation." Luna suddenly realized he had an American accent, and felt a mild glow of pride.

"Well," she shrugged with a smile. Her manager had once said that her smile was charmingly crooked, and had a way of putting those around her at ease. Luna, felt, however, that it often made people underestimate her. She had elfin features, and there were times when people treated her as though she were a child. Luna had learned to play into it, putting people off guard.

"I didn't know Lauren had such high-profile friends," Regan continued.

"Oh, we go way back," Luna said, and Regan nodded, not giving anything away. "Are you on the groom's side?"

"You make it sound like a fight," chuckled Regan. "I'm known to both really, but if I were taking sides, I don't think it would be Prince Michael's."

"They're on the same side now, surely," Luna replied.

"Who knows when it comes to love?" Regan asked, and Luna pursed her lips, wondering what the subtext to that comment was.

II

The church where the wedding was being held was filling up very nicely, as friends of the families took their places on the ornate wooden pews with their soft green cushions. The church was definitely *old*, but the windows around the room were all stained glass, portraying the Stations of the Cross. Those who were inclined ensured they genuflected before taking a seat, but that didn't include Luna, who thought that she would be lucky not to be burned alive when she crossed the threshold. Fortunately, God was feeling generous.

Cameron Regan had taken a place somewhere slightly ahead of her, and as Luna looked around the room, she tried to see if there was anyone else she recognized. There was a haughty looking woman in a purple dress and large hat that seemed vaguely familiar, but aside from that, no one else stood out.

Carefully she moved through the bride's side of the church, and found the seat that had been reserved for her. Already seated was a tall, blonde woman a few years younger than Luna, and she recognized Dana Spectra immediately. Luna didn't often feel intimidated by the company that she was in, but she had to admit on this occasion she was definitely feeling a little inadequate.

"Oh my god, Luna Rochique!" Dana Spectra said in the loudest whisper she thought she could get away with. "I can't believe it's you! I was at your concert last year; you were absolutely amazing!"

"Well, when one of Aussie's top models is gushing over you, it's hard not to be delighted," Luna said, immediately falling into friend mode. She had been aware of Dana's presence at her concert – of course she had, how could she not? The model had been sitting there in the VIP section, dressed in her short black dress with the white collar, and people were surreptitiously trying to take pictures of her. To be fair, the moment Luna had stepped out on stage, Dana's entire attention was on the superstar, but selfishly Luna wanted all the attention to be on her.

That said, she was aware of how ungracious she had felt, and Dana had never done anything to gain her ire, so Luna put her jealously in a box and closed it. Get over yourself, woman, she told herself sternly.

"You totally should have come backstage to meet me," Luna said. "I will make sure you're on the list in future." That bit was true. She was going to try to be a better person.

"I absolutely will," Dana said. "My little sister is the biggest fan of yours. Even bigger than me, and that's saying something."

"Selfie?" Luna asked, and the pair maneuvered to take the picture. Genuine or not, Luna reflected, both of them would benefit from having each other on their socials, and it never hurt to expand the fan base.

Then she paused, blinking.

Surely not?

In the photo, on the groom's side of the church, a man was taking his place to watch the wedding. He was tall, with long curly blonde hair that was streaked with grey. He was wearing an immaculate white suit, though there was a grey dress scarf around his neck, and a beret was perched on his head, with no sign of it being removed. He had a limp, and relied on a wooden cane with a silver handle for support. Luna couldn't see what the handle was, but she didn't have to. She knew exactly who the man was and as such knew that the silver top of the cane was a jaguar's head.

Luna wanted to get up and challenge the man, but she was now boxed into her seat and there was a definite change in the organ music, signalling that the wedding was about to begin. She sat back, nodding an apology to the gentleman on the other side of her, who was clearly getting annoyed with her leaning forward.

What on earth was Professor Axton Beauséjour doing at Lauren's wedding?

III

The wedding was divine.

No, more than that, it was grand. Royal. Over the top, but in a low-key sort of way. This was the Prince of Crovania, and no expense was being spared. But at the same time, this was Crovania, a location that wasn't quite recognized as a country, and therefore with a man who wasn't quite recognized as a prince. But all the same, at the front, resplendent in his black penguin suit and gorgeous red chrysanthemums pinned to his lapel, was royalty.

Prince Michael was undeniably handsome, though he was probably comfortably in his forties, with steel grey hair. There was something very appealing about him, but Luna had to admit she was a little surprised that Lauren had ended up with him. He didn't entirely seem like he would be her type. Though, things change in a decade, and Luna hadn't really kept up with Lauren in the intervening years, so for all she knew maybe she was exactly Lauren's type.

The Prince's best man was maybe the same age as the Prince, but had fought off the grey and was in an even better shape that the Prince. But there was a darkness to him, and his Van Dyke merely made the saturnine features more demonic. There was something about him, though, that suggested he was on edge, as though he wasn't entirely happy with the situation that was unfolding, but ultimately couldn't do anything about it.

That was it, Luna, thought. He had that look on his face as if to say, "Don't say I didn't warn you." He was Cassandra, predicting the downfall of Troy, but being ignored by everyone. She wondered who he was, exactly. Probably some lifelong friend of the Prince's. Hard to tell.

The second groomsman was younger, maybe in his thirties, with a cheery face that was slightly cheeky. Luna found herself wondering what the connection between this guy and the Prince was, because they didn't immediately seem to be besties. He was altogether more fidgety than the other two as well, playing with his lapels and adjusting his tie. It was obviously annoying the best man who turned and whispered something short and sharp, that brought the groomsman back down to Earth.

No love lost between those two, then.

Luna paused for a moment, wondering what she was doing. Why was she trying to analyse the relationships between people. This wasn't normally the sort of thing she did. Yes, she was excessively curious, fascinated to know what was going on, but a deep analysis into people was not something she had done since…well, since anytime she had interacted with Professor Beauséjour. She bit her lip in annoyance, angry that the man's sheer presence was able to alter her way of thinking.

Her last encounter with him hadn't been fantastic, and involved a vicious murder. Was Beauséjour someone who brought Death with him to the parties he attended. Or was Luna just thinking that was what he was like. She sighed. Beauséjour had always made her overthink everything, ever since she had been in his university classes. And then *that*.

Suddenly she realised she had been leaning forward again, annoying the man beside her. She smiled weakly and sat back, but it was only momentary, because as soon as she did, the small little group of musicians on the balcony of the church started playing a bridal march, and everyone stood up in order to get a look at the arrival of the bride down the long red carpet.

Lauren Barton looked gorgeous. The dove white dress was absolutely beautiful, giving an air of mystery to the woman wearing it, while at the same time, making it clear that she was *stunning*.

"That's gotta be Dolce," Dana whispered, and Luna turned to her. "Twenty grand, easy," she added. Not that she was poor by any means, but Luna knew that even she would have questioned that much money being spent on a wedding dress. Or maybe not. Who knows when you actually reach that point to go through with it?

"I'm guessing the bride's family did not pay for the wedding," Luna whispered back, and the two women giggled. Luna was suddenly struck by the fact that Dana was sitting on Lauren's side of the church. Obviously, the woman knew how to mix in the right circles.

There were two bridesmaids, neither of whom Luna recognised.

"Do you know the bridesmaids?" Luna asked Dana.

"Not the chief bridesmaid. The blonde on the end is Kendal Leigh," Dana replied. "She's a model."

"Not Dana level, obviously," Luna grinned, and Dana blushed.

"Well, I don't know," she shrugged. Luna found herself slightly surprised at how much she was enjoying Dana's company, though the man on her other side had clearly had enough, and gave them a sharp hiss to stop them talking.

The bridal party walked down the aisle, Lauren looking ahead without even bothering to see which guests had attended or not. She was probably nervous, Luna supposed, and had to give the woman respect. She was about to do something most people only ever dreamed of; become a princess. Even Luna had to envy that; it was the dream of so many little girls, really.

Kendal Leigh did look like a model, though probably more a swimsuit model, than a catwalk model. She wasn't waifish, but curvy and immediately eye-catching. She and the other bridesmaid were also wearing white, which was surprising, though the bridesmaids' dresses were far simpler than the bride's, being more like satin slips than the gown that the bride was wearing. It was like Coco Chanel had designed the wedding, with nothing more than a few drops of red in the sweeping black and whites.

The chief bridesmaid was older and mousier. She looked nervous, perhaps worried that she might slip up in front of the crowd, or embarrass herself and the bride in the eyes of the world. There was no shortage of photographers at the back of the hall, each with their long-distance lenses to catch every second of the action. Some had even photographed Luna when she walked in, but she was almost becoming desensitized to that sort of thing.

As the organ stopped playing, the room came to a hush, and, surprisingly in English, the priest spoke.

"Dearly beloved…"

Chapter Two

Unexpected Hors d'oeuvres

The Church of The Divine Manifestation, Reidon

I

All around the room, people began to gather their belongings and head out of the Church towards their transportation. For most that was the end of the day. They had seen a royal marriage; Lauren Foster became Princess Lauren of Crovania, and they would talk about it for years to come. Dana and Luna had taken another selfie, posting it on their socials so their followers would see the two celebrities together, and gush over how beautiful they were and how astonishing it was that they knew royalty.

"We should try to get one with Lauren," Luna said. "Imagine that? You, me and a real-life princess. I don't know about you, but my social media guys would be blown away."

"I wish I had social media guys," Dana laughed. "My manager insists that I handle that side of thing, and I am the absolute worst at social media. My little sister does it all for me."

"Oh, I wouldn't trust my little sister with my accounts as far as I could throw her," Luna said, joining in the laughter. "Come on," Luna insisted, grabbing her new friend's hand. "She must still be here, surely? She can't have left just left. They'll be out the back or something. Heading off to photos."

It had been surprising to many of the foreign guests when the royal couple did not head to the front of the church to be photographed together. In fact, the bridal party had gone their separate ways again, with the men heading in one direction and the women heading in another. A big burly man with a bald head and an impressively outdated mustache (though, in fairness, it was an amazing mustache; one which seemed far too bushy to be real, and also sculpted so that it twirled at the ends) had followed the men out, his eyes flashing around the room as he did so, and snapping at two men dressed in black suits, standing inconspicuously near the doorway.

He clearly wasn't hiding the fact he was the head of security, but then, Luna supposed, he probably didn't really need to.

Luna dragged Dana to the side of the building that the Princess had gone through, and both women noticed the security men glancing in their direction as they walked through the private door.

"Come on," Dana said, pulling Luna through another doorway. It was a cupboard, some sort of storeroom for the priest, Luna assumed. Dana was leaning forward to peer through the gap in the door to see what the security guards were doing. As such the taller woman was leaning forward and Luna found herself giggling slightly.

"This is very intimate, Dana. I didn't think we were that close," she said, and put her hands on Dana's waist. The two women burst out laughing, but then quickly put their hands over each other's mouths. The pair peered through the gap again, but there was no sign of security.

"Come no," Luna muttered, slipping out. Before she could do anything, however, Dana grabbed Luna and pulled her back into the closet.

"Look," she whispered softly, and Luna peered through the gap.

Walking down the corridor, resting heavily on every second step, was the curious figure that Luna recognized immediately.

"Who is that?" Dana muttered in Luna's ear, and Luna scowled slightly.

"That is Oxford law professor Axton Beauséjour," Luna replied. They both pushed the door open a little and changed the angle of their viewing so they could see the eccentric figure walk down the corridor. Luna turned to Dana who mouthed a "what do we do?", though the shorter woman shrugged. Setting her jaw, Luna made a decision and exited the little room, then headed down the corridor after Beauséjour. She was aware, and more than a little grateful, that Dana was following her.

They watched as Beauséjour knocked on a door and then went inside. Cautiously, the pair approached the door and paused when they heard voices, though annoyingly they couldn't make out exactly what was being said. Lauren reached for the door, but the door handle started to turn, and Dana grabbed her friend and yanked her into the nearest door they could. This time they found themselves in a toilet, though while Dana was examining their new surroundings, Luna had pulled the door open slightly to watch Beauséjour exit the room.

Once he had moved far enough away, Luna left, and then moved forward and knocked on the door that Beauséjour had gone through.

"Come in," came the call, and Luna turned to see that Dana was once again beside her. The door was opened by a young woman with a pixie quality about her, though there she kept her head somewhat lowered in deference, and the women said thank you as they stepped into the room.

"Lauren?" Dana said hesitantly. Lauren turned to them and stood up, and the both women had to admit their friend looked incredible on her special day. Neither Luna nor Dana were under any illusions about their relationship with Lauren. She had always been slightly resentful that she wasn't in the same spotlights as the other two, and that had created something of a wedge in both relationships. Luna knew exactly why Dana had been hesitant, and she felt the same awkwardness now. However, Lauren had a broad smile on her face, and Luna suspected that she was relishing being the most important girl in the room.

"Oh, oh!" She embraced them both. "I can't believe you both came. I didn't even know you knew each other."

"Oh, we just met today," Luna said.

"I would have put you beside each other at the dinner, but unfortunately Dana isn't staying," Lauren said, and Dana nodded.

"I'm so sorry. I did send my gift on," the model apologized, giving a slight look to Luna.

"It's fine, so fine. I'm just so glad you could make it." Lauren paused, before saying "I don't have a lot of time," and the two other women both nodded. "Should we get a selfie? I'll bet your fans would love to see you with a real-life princess!" It may have been almost identical to what they had thought earlier, but both Luna and Dana exchanged a quick glance thinking exactly the same thing. Princesses didn't have to be humble, they supposed.

The photo was taken and Lauren posted it almost immediately, ensuring that she got the gushing praise immediately.

"Look, I'll see you at the reception," Luna said, providing them an exit.

"And I'll definitely be in touch soon," Dana added.

"So great you could come," Lauren repeated, and suddenly the woman who had opened the door for them had materialized beside them. "Amy will show you out," Lauren added and the dismissal could not have been any more royal.

II

"I'm disappointed you're not going to be at the reception," Luna said to Dana as the door behind them was closed by the maid. Neither of them had grabbed the woman's name, which was probably quite rude all things told, but Luna told herself there were going to be tons of people she would meet today that she wouldn't remember the names of.

"I'm irked," Dana admitted. "But my team have me booked for a function pushing some sports drink, or something. I have to be at a fashion show, or… actually I'm not really sure. I just know that I'm committed to pushing a brand and I'm being paid money to be there."

"I know the feeling," Luna smiled. She turned and looked out of the windows of the church, where they saw a vintage Rolls Royce parked, clearly ready to take the someone to the reception – presumably the bride, given that where they were. The maid had come out with the rather beautiful bouquet that the bride had been carrying, and she opened the door to the Rolls to place it inside. Dione and Kendal were now following, and as they got into the car, the maid had turned and gone back inside.

"Do you think more people are catching up with Lauren?" Dana wondered.

"I wouldn't be surprised," Luna agreed. "There are a lot of people at this wedding who I don't think were invited to the reception afterwards."

"Crovania does big on a small scale," Dana laughed, and Luna joined in. They waited a bit longer, keen to see Lauren head towards the reception, and finally they were rewarded as Lauren walked out of the building, the maid making sure the train of the dress was kept away from the ground.

Then, to her surprise, she saw someone walking up to the bridal party. She didn't look happy, and clearly wanted to have words with Lauren, who was surprisingly alone as her bridesmaids were already in the car.

"Who's that?" Dana wondered aloud. Luna shook her head, completely clueless, but then paused. The woman was wearing purple with an impressive hat, and Luna recalled vaguely seeing the hat earlier at the wedding, but who exactly it belonged to was a mystery.

"I've no idea," Luna said. The pair watched as the conversation seemed to get heated, with both women using expressive hand gestures to make their point. Whatever the conversation was about, it was certainly a passionate topic.

"I wonder why she came to the wedding?"

"That's a very good question," Luna mused. "But then, if I'm honest, I don't think I've seen Lauren in about a decade, so I wonder a little as to what I'm doing here."

"Me too," Dana said with a mixture of surprise and sympathy. "When the invitation came, I was going to throw it away, but everyone suggested it was a good idea to go to a royal wedding, and I had to admit to being curious to catch up with Lauren after all this time." That pretty much summed up everything about her as well, Luna reflected. Did Lauren really have such a great love for them that she invited them, or was she trying to look impressive. And if the latter, why bother? She had just become a princess.

A tall man in a royal blue suit suddenly came over to them. Dana turned to him and sighed heavily, before turning back to Luna.

"This is my keeper," she grinned. "I have to go. I have to admit I'm pretty sad about going now. This whole thing is getting bizarre. But you have my number, right? Let me know what happens." Luna nodded, and the pair leaned hugged.

Luna watched her new friend get escorted from the building by whichever member of her management team was handling her, and then turned to look back through the window. Whatever the conversation had been, Lauren seemed to be upset now, dabbing at her eyes. The two women hugged and then Lauren got into the Rolls and the door shut. The woman in the hat turned and walked away.

Weird, Luna mused.

With that in mind, she headed for the church's exit and her trip to the reception.

The Royal Arms, Reidon

When Luna had discovered that the location of the reception was a place called the Royal Arms, her heart had sunk immediately and she wondered aloud why on Earth any royalty would hold their reception in a pub, of all places.

"It's probably quite a swanky place," her manager, Stone Lennon, had said, trying to buoy her spirits. "Maybe he's one of *those* royals. You know, the type that likes to show they're one of the people. Look at me, I'm like you chaps. I drink in pubs. Except obviously I'm much richer and will never talk to you plebs in a million years." Luna had raised an eyebrow, as Stone chuckled at his own humor, but it was all brought crashing down by her mentor, Egon Maeing, whom Lennon was not a fan of at the best of times.

"I believe," Maeing announced from the armchair he had effectively claimed over the years as his own, "that the Royal Arms was literally a former barracks for the Crovanian regiment that was appointed to serve the King specifically. It's been converted to a reception hall for use by the Royals whenever there is a state function."

"Like a wedding," Luna nodded, and Maeing smiled at her, while Lennon rolled his eyes.

Maeing, however, was absolutely correct. The Royal Arms looked, on the outside, like what it had once been, even if it did have more money spent on it. This one looked like a child had decided to make a building out of bricks, and as such, simply just put a ton on top of another ton. It was rectangular and boring, with lots of windows dotted regularly along the sides. There was a sum total of no imagination put into it, with the exception of the front doors, which were a beautiful mahogany, and the crest of the royal family engraved onto the right, while the army's shield was on the left.

Inside, however, was a very different affair. Entering through the outer doors took you into an antechamber where two footmen, dressed dapperly in their black tailed suits, opened the doors with gloved hands and allowed access directly to the hall beyond. The dining hall was two tables laid out, perpendicular to the head table at which the bridal party sat. On each table, shining cutlery sat beside what was obviously very expensive tableware. Wedgewood? No, probably

Tiffany. And the cutlery was probably Royal Doulton (not, Luna reflected, that she was an expert in these things). Each table had an ornate vase filled with gorgeous white Chrysanthemums, presumably to mirror the bride's bouquet, though there was a single red one in each vase, which made the display more eye catching.

There was, Luna Rochique realised, quite a small collection of people at the reception. The wedding party itself had been huge, with a staggering number of people there, and paparazzi poised on the outside ready to take pictures of whoever they could as they entered and left the church. At the Royal Arms, however, it was a completely different situation. There were no photographers in sight, and the number of guests had been pared back considerably. It was decidedly unlike most royal receptions.

But the rest of the room was something else. Maeing's trivia about it being a former barracks probably explained why the walls had portraits of men with military bearing and incredible mustaches, covered in medals and carrying ceremonial swords and hats. At the end of the hall behind where the married couple and their entourage were sitting, all sorts of weapons were displayed on the wall, from ornate swords to antique muskets. Suits or armour sat in each corner, like sentinels. It was very impressive, all things told. There was a set of doors to the back the room, while on the left wall (as she was standing), was a single door near the back, and on the right, three more doors – though given the waiters exiting with drinks and canapes, Luna guessed she knew where the kitchens were.

What was not so much was Luna's seating placement. She had taken a little wander looking for her name plaque, and realized quickly it wasn't on the table nearest the kitchen. When she explored the other table, she found it and wondered if it was some sort of joke. Sitting at the table already in his place beside her was Professor Axton Beauséjour. For a moment she wondered if she could ask to be moved, but reflected that was probably poor form at a wedding.

Setting her jaw, she walked to her seat and sat down.

"Luna," Beauséjour said, turning to her with a smile. "What a surprise. I don't think I've seen you since." He paused as if trying to remember, but Luna's eyes shot daggers.

"Since you had me arrested!" she said, unable to contain herself.

"What, not since then?" Beauséjour replied, almost genuinely surprised.

"Oh, come on, *Professor*," she snarled.

"Please, just call me Axton," he said.

"I will not, *Professor*. I can't believe you can just sit there…" She petered out, surprisingly quickly, her anger sapping away her ability to speak. In truth, even she was shocked at how angry was with him (which probably came from the fact she had refused to talk about it with him all those years ago).

"I take it you haven't forgiven me," Beauséjour said, and his calm exterior seemed to sadden a little.

"Of course not," she said. "You totally betrayed me!"

"Luna, I told you at the time, I had good reason," he started.

"You could have shared those with me *before* you had me arrested!" Luna snapped. Beauséjour opened his mouth to say something, but then thought better of it and closed it.

"I am sorry, Luna," he said. "I know you don't believe it, but I am." If she were honest, Luna actually did believe him. But that shouldn't give him a pass for being a dick, she decided, folding her arms. "I'm guessing the dinner conversation might be a bit stilted," Beauséjour continued, a smile playing across his lips. Luna scowled.

Professor Axton Beauséjour hadn't really changed all that much in the years she hadn't seen him. There was a timeless quality to him, and she had always struggled to pick his age. He had to have been at least in his thirties when she had studied under him, so that would mean he was comfortably in his forties now, but he certainly didn't look it. He could easily have passed for someone in his thirties, but at times, he could be mistaken for fifty. It was difficult to tell.

He was still wearing his scarf and beret, which was something he always did, and his panther-headed cane was resting against the table beside him. The problem was, she had genuinely adored him when he had been her lecturer. She might even admit to having a crush on the man, who had stood at the front of the lecture hall and made the law sound infinitely more interesting that it actually was. But to then be thrown under the bus by that same someone had hurt as much as the first time she had been dumped by a boyfriend.

Actually, it had hurt more.

She glowered at Beauséjour, who smiled meekly back.

"I see your career has really kicked off," he said, and she frowned more.

"Let's not pretend you're a fan," she muttered.

"I bought *Chaos and Disorder*," he said, and she looked at him, unsure of whether he was telling the truth or not. "I thought it was really good." She opened her mouth to say something, but to her surprise, someone had materialised beside them.

She was a short woman dressed in royal blue with badges, and immediately gave off the vibe of a police officer. Luna wasn't sure exactly what the Crovanian police force wore, but if she were to take a guess, she was going to assume it would be what this woman was wearing.

"Excuse me," she started, her voice clearly betraying her origin. "Are you Professor Axton Beauséjour?"

"Err, yes, I am," Beauséjour replied.

"I was wondering if you could come with me, please?" Luna smirked, secretly hoping he might be placed under arrest. Not that she wanted revenge, but obviously she definitely wanted revenge.

"What's this about?" Beauséjour replied. *Always give the police anything they can easily obtain*, had been Beauséjour's first rule about dealing with the law. *Keep control of the situation*, was his second.

"I'm afraid there's been an incident," the officer replied. "I'm Inspector Dani Kelinaw," she continued (older than she looks, then, Luna reflected).

"I'm not sure how I can help," Beauséjour said, cautiously.

"The Prince asked me to get you personally," Kelinaw said.

"The Prince?" Beauséjour's eyebrows shot up. "Well, I suppose I'd better come. You don't mind if I bring my associate?" To Luna's shock, he turned and indicated her.

"By all means," Kelinaw said, though she was getting more and more agitated. "We need to go."

Beauséjour turned to Luna, the unspoken offer clear. For a moment Luna vacillated between her options. Then, more annoyed at herself than anything else, she stood up. Her curiosity was always going to win.

What could the police possibly want help with at a wedding reception?

Chapter Three

A Small Helping of Murder

The Royal Arms, Reidon

I

"Oh my god," Luna murmured, covering her mouth as she tried to hold back her breakfast. The scene before her was devastating.

They had been taken through the only door on the wall nearest their table, which led to a long corridor, with six doors. The one behind them was clearly an emergency exit, while the one at the end on the corridor was clearly toilets. The second door along the corridor was also for a toilet, which left three doors. Inspector Kelinaw kept walking until they reached the last door before the toilets, and here Prince Michael and the chief bridesmaid stood. The latter was crying, sobbing uncontrollably, while the Prince seemed white and in a state of shock. There was another man there – the big, bald man that Luna had assumed was some sort of security guard from the wedding. Even he looked shaken.

Inspector Kelinaw had stepped through the trio cautiously, beckoning Beauséjour and Luna to follow, and when the door opened, what lay before them explained what had prompted everyone's reactions. The room was an antechamber of sorts – somewhere for the bride to get changed if she were going to, or simply to compose herself. In the middle of the room there was a dresser that almost cut the room in two, complete with a high mirror, presumably allowing the bride the chance to have privacy while she was changing. Just inside the door where two chairs, which Luna assumed were for the bride's guests, whilst Princess Lauren of Crovania sat on a chair behind the mirror.

And she was very dead.

She was no longer wearing her wedding dress, rather she was in, what was probably an exceptionally elegant red dress, but what caught the attention was the blood soaking through the dress, and which seemed to pooling at her feet.

Even more shocking, though, was that it looked like someone had attacked the woman in a frenzy, with knife marks all over the body, from the throat and neck, down the torso and arms, on Lauren's palms, and her legs and even her feet. The body was pale, and Luna guessed there was probably not a drop of blood left in her.

"Exsanguinated," Beauséjour muttered morbidly, and Luna winced.

Standing just beyond the pooling blood was a smartly dressed man with greying hair that was cut fashionably wavy, and a mustache that was very impressive. He was hard to pitch the age of, given that he didn't look particularly old, but the mustache seemed so old-fashioned it dated him tremendously.

He looked up as Beauséjour and Luna entered, taking off his glasses and sliding them into his top pocket.

"Ah," he said. "A break in the deadlock?"

"Sorry?" Beauséjour asked, but Luna noticed that he was looking around the room intently.

"There's a deadlock. Between the dear Inspector and Mr Burton out there." The man waved at the door, and Luna turned to see no one else had followed them in.

"What sort of a deadlock?" she asked, curiously.

"Oh, I don't know details," the man said, sniffily.

"Who are you?" Beauséjour raised an eyebrow.

"Dr Fabian Kilman, at your service," he said, stretching out a hand, which Axton Beauséjour failed to take. Luna leaned forward and shook it. "Personal physician to the Prince," he added confidentially to Luna.

"Did you examine the body?" Beauséjour turned to Kilman, suddenly interested in the man.

"Not up close, I…" Kilman waved at the blood on the ground, and Beauséjour nodded approvingly.

"So, you didn't make those?" Beauséjour pointed to a set of footprints in the blood, and Luna chided herself for not noticing them.

"No, I most certainly did not!" Beauséjour looked querulously at Kilman, and used his walking stick to prod at Kilman's shoes. Kilman scowled, but lifted a foot, one by one, to prove his point. "Satisfied?"

"No," Beauséjour murmured.

"He means with this," Luna said, indicating the room, and Kilman nodded. "If you didn't examine the body, I'm assuming you don't have a cause of death?"

"Well, I think it's relatively obvious," Kilman said, and pointed at the corpse. Luna winced slightly, and was inclined to agree with what Kilman was saying. Beauséjour, on the other hand, seemed distracted. He frowned slightly, and turned to look around the room, before turning back to Kilman, his eyebrow raised again.

"Hazard a guess at the time of death?" Beauséjour posed.

"Oh, well, it's hard to tell. That sort of wound wouldn't leave her alive for too long. Ten minutes at most to bleed out, I would have said. At most."

"Interesting," Beauséjour said. "Thank you, Doctor Kilman. I think you can go."

"I beg your pardon?" Kilman asked, his voice full of outrage.

"If I have any further questions for you, I'll let you know," Beauséjour added. Kilman's jaw dropped for a moment, but he moved out of the room with as much dignity as he could muster. Luna took out her phone and started to snap photos of the room. While she did, Inspector Kelinaw and the aforementioned Mr Burton, stepped in, apparently determined to demonstrate how different they could be. "So?" Beauséjour said to them.

"We would like to investigate what has happened, but," Kelinaw began, but before the short woman could finish, her much larger companion jumped in.

"This is a royal murder," Burton exclaimed. "This is not an investigation for the local plods!"

"Who are you?" Luna asked pointedly.

"Solomon Burton, head of security," Burton snapped, and Luna decided immediately she didn't like him.

"So why call him?" Luna asked, jerking her thumb in Beauséjour's direction.

"The Prince has vouched for him," Burton replied, and he seemed suddenly very sulky.

"Apparently Professor Beauséjour is an expert in this field," Kelinaw added, and Luna narrowed her eyes, before looking at Beauséjour who gave her a weak smile. "We're happy for Professor Beauséjour to start investigations, but obviously we will have to make any final arrest."

"I trust the Prince's judgement," Burton said, though he gave the impression he absolutely did not.

"Thank you," Beauséjour said politely. "I can't really promise anything. I think the Prince may be overselling my abilities," he continued, but Luna interjected.

"Oh please," she muttered. "He'll find your killer, no matter what the cost." She gave him another look, and he had the audacity to look hurt.

"I will do my best," he agreed, and Kelinaw looked a little relieved. "Do you mind if we have the room?" This time neither Kelinaw nor Burton seemed particularly happy, but they both stepped out. Beauséjour went to the door and closed it, before turning back to the room.

"What do you notice?" he asked, and Luna gave him a look, before turning to look at the room.

"I guess she came here to get changed into a new dress," Luna speculated.

"And someone cut her rather severely," Beauséjour added unnecessarily.

"After she got changed. Are we looking for clues?"

"Yeah," Beauséjour nodded.

Luna looked around the room, having put her phone away. She could see the wedding dress hanging from the back wall. The Princess was completely dressed...

"She would have been helped in getting changed by her bridesmaids and her personal maid, right?" Beauséjour nodded at Luna. "So, they left, and then the murderer slipped in."

"The murderer walks in, and comes up behind the Princess," Beauséjour mused, and cautiously moved around the pool of blood, surprisingly agile for someone with a walking stick. As he stood behind the Princess, his eyes widened slightly, and Luna quickly skipped around the blood to stand close to her former mentor. When she did, she understood why Beauséjour had seemed surprised. On the mirror, there was an "R" scrawled in blood.

"Lauren used her own blood to identify her killer," Luna muttered.

"R...for Rochique?" Beauséjour turned to look at Luna, a slight smile on his lips. She glared at him.

"Or maybe she was trying to write something else but lost the energy. Maybe a B...for Beauséjour!"

"Touche," grinned Beauséjour.

"You already blame me?"

"Did you see her when you arrived at the reception?"

"No!" exclaimed Luna. "I went pretty much straight to the hall. What about you?"

"Same," Beauséjour said. "Shall we agree that neither of us killed Princess Lauren?"

"Well, I wasn't the one pointing fingers," sulked Luna.

"Good point."

"But presumably the R...or B must mean something," Luna said.

"Yes," Beauséjour replied, but seemed strangely non-committal.

"You don't think so?"

"It seems overly dramatic, don't you think? I mean, if you were bleeding to death, would you pause to draw the initial of your killer in blood?"

"I'd call for an ambulance," Luna shrugged.

"Exactly. You don't have much time, so why waste it?" Luna pointed to the table, where there was a set of white gloves on it, stained with blood.

"The killer's?" she wondered.

"But no sign of the murder weapon," Beauséjour noted. "The killer... pocketed it? But took time to take off the gloves." He pointed to the table where there were a pair of clearly blood-stained white gloves. Luna didn't like the theory, but was happy to see that Beauséjour clearly wasn't keen on it either. The two carefully moved back to the other part of the room, avoiding the blood pool again. "She's been dead for a little while, I think," Beauséjour said.

He paused for a moment, and crouched down to the ground, something clearly catching his attention. Luna watched as he examined a white flower that had fallen, and that seemed to be made of glass, but it was clearly badly damaged.

"Important?" Luna asked.

"No," Beauséjour said. "Though clearly the killer wasn't careful. They either hadn't planned to kill, or they needed to be quick. Probably time to chat to those that found the body."

II

Prince Michael, grey haired, sombre and austere, wearing his black suit, and the red chrysanthemum, as well as a wonderful collection of medals on the sash sweeping up over his shoulder, was waiting for Beauséjour and Luna as the pair exited the room. The chief bridesmaid was also with him still, but she was an emotional wreck, unable to do anything except put her head in her hands and weep. Luna got the impression Beauséjour was somewhat annoyed with her.

"I'm sorry, Professor," the Prince was saying. "I didn't mean to drag you into this, but this is my wife, for god's sake. I can't have the police and my security fighting about who is going to find the killer and nothing get done. I thought you were the best option."

"It's fine, don't worry," Beauséjour said, a little magnanimously, Luna though drily. She'd forgotten about the Professor's ego. "Did you find the Princess?"

"Well, yes, me and Dione," the Prince replied, indicating the bridesmaid.

"Dione?"

"Dione Lora," the woman said between sobs.

"So, the two of you discovered the Princess, because…?" Beauséjour let the question hang in the air.

"She was taking some time," Prince Michael said. "I had expected her a lot earlier, but I knew she was getting changed." Beauséjour looked like he was about to say something, but instead remained silent, letting the Prince continue. "I sent Hunter to get her, and I'm not sure exactly what happened, but the next thing I know, Pero is telling me that the door is locked and she's not responding. So, Dione and I came down, and he was right. We got Burton to open the door and…" The Prince choked off at this, but Beauséjour didn't seem to notice.

"Hunter and Pero?"

"Pero Petar is my best man and Hunter Shelby is my other groomsman."

Beauséjour looked up and down the corridor as though looking for something, and Luna wondered if he thought they might find security cameras in the place. The Royal Arms, however, seemed designed for discretion for the royal family, and so no one was keeping an eye on them.

"Did you knock? You knocked and she didn't answer?" Beauséjour said, his attention suddenly zooming back in on Prince Michael.

"Yes, we called out and got no response."

"And then when you opened the door, you went in and…everything was as it was," Beauséjour said.

"Yes, yes. I sent Dione to get Dr Kilman, and when he came back, he told us the diagnosis."

"Hardly a diagnosis," Beauséjour muttered. Dione continued to cry, and this time Luna could definitely see the annoyance on Beauséjour's face.

"Hey, come with me, and we'll get some water," Luna said, taking the woman's hand. Dione appreciatively took it and headed up the corridor with Luna. Beauséjour watched them go before turning back to the Prince.

"Did you step in the blood?"

"What?" Prince Michael looked astonished.

"When you went to check on Lauren, did you step in the blood? Are those your footprints?" Michael looked at him a little surprised, before shaking his head.

"No," he said. "No definitely not." Michael reached up and smoothed his already very smooth moustache before continuing. "No, I couldn't. I just couldn't. I was…very shocked."

"You walked in, you saw the blood and the knife wound and you were horrified, so you turned to Ms Lora and told her to summon Dr Kilman, and then…you stood there?"

"I think I was in shock," Prince Michael replied, smoothing his moustache again. Beauséjour looked up and down the corridor again, still seeking out something that was not apparent, but again he refused to elaborate.

"You should go have a cup of sweet tea," Beauséjour said. "It'll help with the shock." Prince Michael nodded at him, and then turned and walked up the corridor, back towards the main dining area. Beauséjour followed him a little, but stopped when he realised he had passed by the toilet door. He knocked, and then called in: "Luna?"

"Here," Luna said, coming out of the portal, followed by Dione Lora. Dione wasn't an unattractive woman, but there was something very ordinary about her. She had a round face, but it was a little long, and her hair was parted in the centre and pulled down on either side, giving her the unfortunate appearance of wearing a wig, or perhaps a black bonnet.

"Can I ask, Ms Lora?" Beauséjour began, clearly going to ask regardless of what the answer to the question was. "What did you see when you stepped into the room?"

"Sorry?" the woman replied, her voice a mixture of shock and confusion. "What did I see?"

"Yes, sorry, I mean…I suppose I mean, you didn't step in the blood, did you?"

"What blood?" Beauséjour frowned at her, and even Luna turned in surprise.

"You can't have missed the blood," Luna said.

"Where was the blood?"

"It was on the floor," Beauséjour replied, genuinely puzzled. "You didn't see the blood?"

"Well, I was shaken. I didn't go near the body. I was just too shocked. So, I must have missed it."

"Not your footprints, then," Beauséjour murmured.

"They were clearly not heels," Luna said pointedly, and Beauséjour nodded at her.

"I was mostly useless," Dione whimpered, and Luna was worried Beauséjour might agree with her.

"You've had quite the shock, Ms Lora," Beauséjour said. "You should go back to the hall and have something sweet. It will help."

"I'm just so…" She burst into tears again, and Luna hugged her, while Beauséjour patted her on the back reassuringly. After a few awkward moments, Dione went back to the hall, not really having shaken off the tears. As the doors closed, Luna turned to Beauséjour.

"How could she not have seen the blood?" she asked excitedly. Beauséjour shrugged.

"Some people don't look at their feet when they walk," he said.

"And I saw you looking for security cameras," Luna added.

"I wasn't looking for security cameras," Beauséjour replied.

"Oh," Luna felt a little deflated. "Well, why were you looking up and down the corridor?"

"I was wondering if there was somewhere the murderer might have hidden the knife," Beauséjour replied, and Luna "aahhhed" appreciatively.

"The other rooms?" and Luna pointed to the other doors. Experimentally, Beauséjour walked to the nearest door they hadn't tried, but it remained firmly locked. The other door was just as stubborn, and when Luna went to the end of the corridor, the entrance to those toilets was, surprisingly also locked.

"The emergency exit is alarmed, so that clearly wasn't opened," Beauséjour noted.

"Maybe they flushed it down the toilet," Luna suggested cheekily.

"Knives don't tend to flush well," replied Beauséjour, missing the joke. Suddenly he moved past her and into the toilet, and to Luna's surprise wrestled with the top of the cistern of the sole toilet that was there. With a grunt he succeeded, his walking stick hanging in the crook of his arm, and Luna joined him as they looked inside, providing more light with her phone torch.

"Disappointed," Lun asked.

"An easy answer is always preferable," he replied. "Because this means…" and Luna cut him off before he could finish.

"Whoever the killer is, still has the weapon on him!"

"No," Beauséjour shook his head. "He – or she or they – have had more than ample opportunity to lose the knife, or whatever it was."

"Oh yeah, I suppose," Luna deflated again, annoyed at how Beauséjour could do that.

"Dinner?"

Luna stared at him.

III

When Beauséjour put his hand on the door handle, he was slightly surprised to find it flung open in his face, and even Luna took a step back, drawing in a surprised breath.

Before them, his bald head gleaming with sweat, and still looking distinctly uncomfortable in his suit, was the head of security, Burton.

"Bloody hell," breathed Luna. "You scared the living…" She refrained, suddenly conscious of being at a royal wedding. Oh, and royal murder.

"Mr Burton?" Beauséjour asked and Burton looked at them imperiously.

"Yes?" It was a definite question and Luna unconsciously took a step back, bringing her slightly behind Beauséjour. There was something a little terrifying about Burton, and Luna wondered if the big man was a powder keg waiting to go off.

"Can I ask you a few questions?" Luna had to admire Beauséjour's gall. She wouldn't want to have asked anything of Burton, let alone questions that might suggest they blamed him for the murder.

Please be tactful!

"Solomon Burton," the man replied, snappily. "I am head of security."

"Yes, I remember. You're not Crovanian are you?" Beauséjour wondered.

"No," the guard replied. "English. I was recruited by the Prince a few years ago when he was studying in the UK. You were his lecturer, weren't you? I remember you."

"Ah, yes," Beauséjour nodded. "I'm not that important. Can you please tell me what the security arrangements were for this particular corridor?"

"I myself was standing guard at this door. It's the only access to the corridor."

"Aside from the emergency exit and the toilets at the end of the corridor," Beauséjour said.

"That's an access?" Luna asked.

"There's an entrance to those toilets both in this corridor and in the main hall," Beauséjour said, and Dana realised they must have been beside the main entrance. Oh, she mused, as the layout of the building fell into place. That's what was on either side of the lobby.

"No," Burton interrupted. "All doors in this corridor not being used by the Princess were locked. It was part of the deal with the management. The only way into this corridor was passed me, and that's why I know exactly who the killer was."

"Sorry?" Luna and Beauséjour found themselves saying at the same time.

"That's right. I know who the killer was. Is. Whatever." Burton thrust his bottom jaw forward, and his eyes almost bulged out of his head. He was even able to make his moustache prickle, like some sort of crazed walrus.

"Would you care to enlighten me?" Beauséjour asked.

"You will steal my thunder. And I'm not going to help you. You can work it out on your own." Burton folded his eyes, and Luna suddenly found herself very annoyed.

"Are you a child?" she asked, unable to contain her annoyance.

"I will not let the killer go, because I know who it is. But the Prince believes you can do a better job than me, so I will not get in your way. I'll answer all your questions. But I won't give away my trump card."

"Right," Beauséjour said, hesitantly. "So, you guarded this corridor. Anyone who came down here definitely passed by you."

"Correct," Burton said, and he suddenly seemed unjustifiably proud of himself. "And no one carried a weapon when they walked down this corridor, because I would have seen."

"So, no one came down this corridor with a gun or a knife," Beauséjour said, and Burton sneered at him. "Or," Beauséjour continued, "a salt shaker. Maybe a drink."

"A salt shaker?" Burton asked, a little confused. "What are you talking about?"

"Oh, poison in the salt," Luna said, suddenly seeing the connection.

"That's not a weapon," protested Burton. "I meant a *weapon*. A… weapon." It was a lame finish to a sentence, but Luna knew that Beauséjour had lost all respect for the man, anyway.

"It's good to know that we have you around to protect us from all forms of danger," Beauséjour said, but the jibe was obvious.

"I will have you know," Burton snarled, grabbing Beauséjour by the jacket lapel, "that I would give my life for the royal family. That's how much I love them."

"Including the Princess?" Beauséjour asked and Burton let him go.

"What do you mean?"

"Well, I just mean, you could argue she wasn't part of the Royal Family. Do you argue that, maybe?" Burton seemed shaken, and his eyes widened, slightly panicked.

"Well, yes," he started, but then stopped. "I mean, no, I don't argue that she wasn't part of the Royal Family."

"That doesn't surprise me," Beauséjour said smoothly.

"Wait," Burton paused, replaying the conversation in his head, "No, I meant to say I do argue that she is part of the Royal Family. I mean, I argue that she is. Not isn't. I don't argue that she isn't." Burton had started to babble, and rather smoothly, both Beauséjour and Luna pushed past him on either side, getting to the door behind Burton. Beauséjour pushed it open, standing back.

"Perhaps you need a rest, Mr Burton?" Beauséjour suggested, and Luna smirked. The pair exited, leaving the security guard somewhat furious behind.

Chapter Four

In Which at Least One Person Attempts To Deceive Axton Beauséjour

The Royal Arms, Reidon

I

Dinner had been served, which was unexpected, and Luna wondered if anyone had told the staff about the murder. Given the way everyone was tucking into the entrée, Luna extrapolated on that idea and wondered if the murder had been broached by anyone while she and Beauséjour had been completing their examinations.

Even Axton Beauséjour himself had seemed to forget about the murder and was tucking into the shrimp-on-rice entrée that had been served up.

"How can you eat at a time like this?" Luna hissed.

"Crovania is renowned for its shrimp," Beauséjour replied between mouthfuls. "You should try it. It's incredible. The sauce is to die for." Luna shook her head, unable to believe her eyes. Though, she reflected, that being said, the entrée did look incredible. And it wasn't like *not* eating it would bring Lauren back to life.

Before she could take a bite, however, the short form of Inspector Danielle Kelinaw appeared and clapped. She had a surprisingly impressive way of commanding attention, Luna reflected, as the short woman clapped a second time. Everyone's attention was now on the police inspector.

"Forgive me for interrupting you. Please, remain seated. It is with great sadness that I must inform you that Princess Lauren of Crovania has been found dead. We are currently investigating the crime, but as you can imagine, this will take some time. As such, I am telling you that you cannot leave this building and must remain here until the investigation is complete. If you attempt to leave, you will be arrested. I shall be taking no further questions at this point. This is a police matter now."

There was hardly any surprise at the immediate babble of voices, which clearly sounded like it was swinging between confusion and outrage. Luna glanced at Beauséjour who shrugged a little.

"I didn't think the Inspector would break it like that," Luna whispered.

"There's no point in keeping it a secret I suppose," Beauséjour replied. "Though, given that she can't investigate, I wonder if she's just making a point to Burton." Luna glanced across at the big man who looked absolutely livid. As Luna looked around the room, she was intrigued by the different looks on the faces at the tables. The Prince at his main table, seemed distressed, and Dione Lora looked as though she were on the verge of losing control, once again. Curiously, the best man just seemed imperious, barely able to register any sort of emotion, while the other groomsman was badly shaken. The other bridesmaid, however, looked lost in thought.

An odd response.

Luna nudged Beauséjour and indicated the bridesmaid, but the professor just shook his head.

"People respond differently to trauma," he said dismissively.

"So, she gets a pass?"

"No, not at all. She just doesn't leap to the top of the suspect list because she isn't crying her eyes out." Luna scowled slightly, the past still fresh in her mind.

"I can't believe we have to sit here and do nothing," someone exclaimed, though Luna wasn't sure who it was. There were murmurings of agreement to this statement, and when someone stood up, Luna felt a slight chill run through her. Over time she had become something of an expert judging the moods of a crowd. Whether she played to tens or tens of thousands, you could feel the vibe of the room, feel when people were getting restless, and feel when people were getting frustrated. Everyone would know that feeling here, but Luna could see the frustration was about to turn to negative action.

"Wait," she blurted out, without thinking. "We aren't going to sit here and do nothing." The people in the room looked at her with a mixture of curiousity and confusion. Being the centre of attention was not a new experience for the rock star, and as all eyes focussed on her, she felt she was in her element. She could easily take control of the crowd. "Don't panic. After all, it's not like we don't have someone who can point us in the right direction. We are joined by famed detective Professor Axton Edevane Sam Beauséjour." Her reveal was laced with sarcasm, and Beauséjour looked at her in surprise.

"I'd hardly say famed Ms Rochique," he replied, a little uncomfortably.

"Oh, don't be so coy, Professor. I know who you are and what you've done. And I'm definitely not the only one," said Luna. She looked over to the Prince with a meaningful glance, and it was not lost on the rest of the room. She could feel the sense of respect for Beauséjour swell slightly, and was a little pleased with herself.

"Don't forget, I could be a suspect," Beauséjour said softly. "Suspect everybody," he added.

"When did you last see Princess Lauren?" Luna demanded. Beauséjour's eyebrows furrowed as he wondered where the singer was going.

"Admittedly I haven't spoken to her today. I arrived late at the wedding, and have not had a chance to talk to her at the reception."

"You could be lying," someone said, and Luna turned to see an older man in a steel grey suit speaking. The suit seemed to have been made to match the man's hair and eyes, and there was a strong no-nonsense vibe about him.

"He is lying," the younger bridesmaid suddenly said. "You saw Lauren just before we left for the reception. You were pretty much the last person to actually see her!" Luna turned to look at Beauséjour, her face a mixture of surprise, and Beauséjour himself shook his head.

"I apologise," Beauséjour said. "By today, I meant the reception. Thank you for correcting me. It looks like we all need to be careful about what we say and how we say it." His words were directed at the grey man, who seemed a little cowed by this. "There's no reason we couldn't do a little digging of our own, I suppose," Beauséjour continued, standing up from his chair. Luna noted that he had finished off his entrée. "Perhaps it might be appropriate if I got the chance to chat with everyone one-on-one? Would anyone object to that, particularly?"

Everyone looked at each other, but no one was prepared to outright say anything objectionable.

"I think that would be entirely appropriate, Professor," the Prince said, and this was enough to end any resistance in the group. The Prince had spoken and everyone would fall into line as a consequence.

"May we know how Princess Lauren passed away?" the grey man asked.

"You are?" Beauséjour looked at him.

"Clayton Reese," the man replied. "I'm a friend of Lauren's family."

"We *are* Lauren's family," the woman beside him said.

"Oh," Beauséjour clicked his fingers. "You gave her away."

"I've been her father since my old friend passed away." Clayton Reese seemed a little upset at this, and the woman beside him touched his arm. She was much less grey, dressed in a peach number that was complimented by Clayton Reese's pocket square, which was in the same colour. Mrs Reese, presumably, Luna reflected.

"It's not pleasant, Mr Reese," Beauséjour said, which Luna thought was uncharacteristically sensitive of him.

"And who found her?" Mrs Reese asked.

"I did," the Prince said, and he almost choked on his words. There was an intake of breath around the room as everyone took in the consequences of his words, and felt his pain. Except Beauséjour, Luna noted. His eyes were flickering around the room, trying to take in the expressions of everyone that was there.

"I think," Beauséjour said, "it would be better if I chatted to people outside of this setting. I don't think we'll get anywhere with everyone concerned about what others might hear."

"You think we're hiding something?" a voice asked, and Luna recognised it immediately. Cameron Regan was sitting back in his chair, his eyes boring into Beauséjour, though the older man seemed unimpressed.

"Everyone's hiding something, Mr Regan," Beauséjour replied, and Luna saw that Regan was surprised that Beauséjour knew him by name. "It will all come out in the wash, I suspect."

Regan wasn't the only one in the room that exchanged a glance with someone else. Beauséjour was right, Luna reflected. The question was, how far would those who had something to hide go in order to keep it hidden?

II

"Shouldn't we be doing some more investigating of the crime scene? Maybe find some more clues? Surely those things are important?" Luna asked, as Beauséjour walked around the room that the pair now found themselves in. It was something of an antechamber to the hall where everyone was dining in, beside the kitchen if Luna had got the hang on the layout of the building correct. Outside, everyone would presumably be asking questions of each other, which Luna sort of wished she was taking part in. Though she knew that if anything exciting was going to happen, Axton Beauséjour would be involved.

Inspector Danielle Kelinaw was also with them, looking put upon, though exactly who by was a mystery. Beauséjour had wondered if there was a room they might be able to talk to people individually, and Kelinaw had suggested this room. Given the location, though, Luna wondered if it was significant; they couldn't be further away from the crime scene now, which made her wonder, did Kelinaw want them as far away as possible? It was hard to tell, but Beauséjour didn't seem put out, and had even taken Kelinaw aside and whispered a few words in her ear. The Inspector's eyes had lit up at whatever she had been told and when she was about to open her mouth, Beauséjour simply shook his head and then nodded.

"Who," Beauséjour said, "do you think we should start with?" He looked directly at Luna, and the singer narrowed her eyes suspiciously.

"Why are you asking me?"

"Why not?" Beauséjour grinned.

"I never know what you're thinking," Luna pouted, sitting down in front of the law professor.

"You look lovely in that outfit," Beauséjour replied, and Luna narrowed her eyes even more.

"What's that supposed to mean?"

"Nothing more than a compliment," Beauséjour answered.

"Yes, but *why*," Luna said. "Why this sudden asking me about my opinions and telling me how lovely I look?"

"Maybe I'm trying to build a better trust between us," Beauséjour said, and this time the smile seemed genuine. Luna frowned, still not sure whether she trusted Beauséjour or not. Her outfit was divine, however, that was true, and she was glad someone had noticed it. She had flicked her team a few messages during the service to see if the paparazzi had gotten any inappropriate photographs thanks to the slit, a constant worry she had getting out of cars these days. One small flash of underwear and suddenly she was the headline of some stupid social media clickbait. She loved the fans, and could even tolerate their distaste of anything new, because at least it showed how passionate about things they were. The paparazzi, on the other hand, were awful, and she would be happy if they disappeared from the Earth completely.

What she did like about her outfit, was how it showed off the tattoos on her leg. There were times she was so used to her body art she forgot about it, and when asked, she wondered how people could not know, before remembering she had covered it up for whatever reason. Today she decided to show it off, and her outfit, which also included an amazing backless jacket, ensured that everything on her legs and back was on display to the world.

"Well, I'm glad you like it, I suppose," she grumbled.

"You almost stole the show from the bride," Inspector Kelinaw said, and Luna turned with a smile, before suddenly swinging back to Beauséjour.

"You're trying to find out if I had any beef with Lauren?" she snapped. "In a fairly insidious way, I might add. No, I didn't wear this outfit to steal the thunder because I had some long grudge with her, and before you go any further, we slept together years ago. OK? I'm not hiding anything, and if you want to establish a trust between us, maybe you could try by being sincere, *Professor*!"

Furious that she had been duped, she stood up, to storm out, but was surprised to find Beauséjour's hand on her arm. It was a restraint, but it was gentle and there was no pressure, but it made her turn.

"Actually, I genuinely thought you looked beautiful. I didn't for one minute assume you were trying to upstate the bride. I don't think you're the killer, Luna. Please." Not for the first time, Luna Rochique found herself frustrated by Axton Beauséjour. As usual, he made her want to believe him, but she still couldn't shake what happened in the past.

And yet she wanted to trust him.

Sighing, she sat down in the chair.

"The Prince," she said, and Beauséjour looked at her. "That's who I want to talk to first. The Prince."

"Inspector, could you make that happen, please? Oh, and the guest list." Kelinaw looked at him, and again Luna saw something pass between them – a look that conveyed a greater message. The Inspector turned and left the room to retrieve their first guest.

III

In the Hall, the guests were struggling with what to do and what to say. Meals had been brought out to be eaten, and some had opted to begin, but others thought it was in bad taste, and some felt that they should wait until the Prince began before they did. The Prince, however, was clearly not interested in eating, and that made things even more awkward.

"You should eat, Michael." Prince Michael turned to his best man, with surprise.

"How on earth do you think I can eat, Pero?" he asked, and Lord Pero Petar shrugged a little.

"I know it's hard, but it might calm you down a little," said Hunter Shelby, the other male member of the bridal party.

"I don't think I could calm down," Prince Michael replied miserably.

"I have to know," Pero said, and he lowered his voice a little, "are you really sure it is a good idea to let this Professor Beauséjour take on the investigation?"

"You saw the issues between the police and Burton," Prince Michael said.

"I know, but to take it away from Crovanian authorities of any description and hand it to some random wedding guest," Lord Pero spat.

"He was my former law professor," Prince Michael said. "I trust him with my life, Pero!"

"I'm aware," Lord Pero said. "You most certainly are in this situation."

"What does that mean?"

"Your throne was dependent on a bride, Michael. You have no bride," Pero pointed out.

"That's callous," Hunter replied, and Pero turned to him, giving the impression of a hawk suddenly seeing a sparrow.

"Unlike you," Lord Pero whispered, "I have to think about the things that no one else will. And Prince Michael is bound by tradition, which he may have forgotten about, but which I have not. I have to take care of these things."

"You're not a councillor or Chancellor, Pero," Hunter sighed.

"No more fighting, please," Prince Michael commanded. "This is a hard enough time without my two closest friends bickering. I will do what must be done, but tonight, I feel I am entitled to grieve."

"Of course," Pero muttered, and Hunter also lowered his head.

"Your highness?" The three men turned to look behind them, where Inspector Danielle Kelinaw was standing. "Would it be possible for you to come this way, please. Professor Beauséjour would like to speak with you." For a moment, Michael seemed puzzled, and he and his groomsmen glanced at each other in confusion. Finally, Prince Michael nodded. "Of course." He stood up, and followed Kelinaw, the ape-like figure of Solomon Burton shadowing them.

IV

"Do you think he's a suspect?" Luna asked Beauséjour, who had taken out a little book and was writing in it.

"Everybody's a suspect," he said blithely, and Luna scowled.

"I'm still a suspect, despite everything?"

"I didn't mean that," Beauséjour replied evenly, putting the book down to look at her. "But we're at a wedding. Everyone here has some relationship with the bride and groom in some way, and everybody has a past. There are hidden secrets, things that have niggled at people, though they've never actually spoken about it. The greater the fame, the bigger the niggles have become. It's a fairly small group of people out there for a wedding for anyone. I find it difficult to believe that they all get along."

"Including you?"

"Well," Beauséjour started, and then grinned. "I'm the exception that proves the rule."

"And me?"

"Two exceptions," he offered, and Luna opened her mouth to retort, but the arrival of the Prince interrupted her. She was already standing, but she noticed that Beauséjour didn't bother. Behind the Prince there was someone else – tall, bald, with a white moustache, the man was dressed like a traditional butler.

If it looks like a duck and quacks like a duck, Luna reflected.

"Professor, I am very glad you are here, and so glad you're helping," the Prince said. He stepped forward to shake Beauséjour's hand, which brought him close to Luna, who didn't move. "I don't think we've been formally introduced," he said.

"Luna Rochique. I'm a friend of your…" She paused, uncertain what to say, and sure enough the pain on the Prince's face was enough. "I'm sorry for your loss," she added.

"Thank you," he replied, and sat down. Luna wondered where the chair had come from and then realised the butler had provided one. A proper gentleman's gentleman, she reflected. Suddenly it struck her that she was very close to royalty, and she took a quick look around, wondering if Solomon Burton was nearby as well, ready to rush to the Prince's defence if something untoward should happen to him. She couldn't see him, but perhaps he was better at his job than she thought. Or perhaps this place was so well protected, and the guests so well vetted that everything inside was regarded as safe.

Or perhaps he just wasn't a very good bodyguard.

"You're a singer, am I correct?" She nodded at the Prince. "I think I've heard your music. You're very talented. I'm not sure why the Professor has recruited you…"

"She was also one of my students," Beauséjour supplied.

"Ah, well. How quickly we are replaced as teacher's pet," the Prince smiled, and Luna couldn't tell exactly what he was driving at.

"I'm definitely not teacher's pet," she replied, and was surprised at the brief look of hurt that crossed Beauséjour's face. He was right, she reflected. You never knew exactly what other people were thinking.

"Michael, you weren't with Lauren when you were studying under me. When did you meet her?"

"Oh, it must have been about the time I was studying with you. About three years ago, maybe? I was invited to a night out for some reason or another, and Dione insisted she would bring her friend, Lauren with her. It was all very uncomfortable for me, as you can imagine. I don't really do a lot of partying, especially these days. But we got talking and she was quite fascinating. I think I fell in love with her immediately. She was very alluring." He paused, drifting back to the past, presumably, as there was a faint smile on his lips. "I thought we had forever."

"Sadly, that's something we never have," Beauséjour sighed.

"Oh," the Prince suddenly said. "I'm a suspect." He looked as though the thought had never crossed his head, and Luna supposed that it probably hadn't for a couple of reasons. It must be nice to live in that world, under the impression that everything you did was beyond reproach.

"Everyone's a suspect," she said, a little snarkily, but Michael just nodded. Beauséjour's rules were known to everyone who had studied with him.

"You were wearing gloves at the wedding," Beauséjour suddenly said, and the Prince's eyes widened in surprise.

"Well, yes, that's very true," he agreed.

"But not now."

"I took them off earlier," the Prince said, and his voice was very measured.

"Forgive me sire, but I have access to his highness' gloves if they are required," the butler suddenly said.

"Beddows, my butler," the Prince said.

"Ah," Beauséjour exhaled. "Also, to the Princess?"

"The Princess had her own maid. Birkman. I did attend to her on occasion, but rarely had need to." Beddows didn't meet Beauséjour's eyes, but this seemed lost on the professor.

"Did you have need today?"

"The Princess did request I bring her a drink, yes," Beddows replied laconically. Beauséjour opened his mouth to say something, and then closed it again.

"This will be a process, of course Michael," Beauséjour said, standing up, and Luna noticed Beddows cringed when Beauséjour used the Prince's name casually. She also noticed that the Prince was flustered by Beauséjour's dismissal. He was probably not really used to it, she reflected.

"Oh yes, of course," the Prince nodded. There was no hand shaking, no further discussion. The interview was over. For now. The Prince exited the room, followed by his butler, and Luna turned to Beauséjour, but before she could say anything, Beauséjour was talking.

"Those photos of the room, can I see them please?" he asked, and Luna took out her phone and handed it over to him.

"What?" she asked. He handed the phone back to her.

"What do you notice?" he asked.

"Uhm, it's a bloody mess?"

"Outside of that."

"Uhm.." Suddenly she felt like she back in Beauséjour's class, being given an assignment that she wasn't sure she even knew how to start. "What should I be looking for?"

"No glass," he said. "The Princess requested a drink from Beddows, but no glass. Or mug."

"So, he took it away? He's very efficient."

"Which means he saw her three times that afternoon." Beauséjour started to count off on his fingers. "He was asked to get her a drink. He brought her a drink. Then he took the cup away. Three times."

"Well, he was probably just assuming we'd take that for granted."

"Nothing should be taken for granted in a murder investigation."

Yes. She almost forgot that rule.

Chapter Five

One Or Two Surprising Discrepancies

The Royal Arms, Reidon

I

Luna tried to tell Beauséjour that when he called for Dione Lora, he was definitely going to get someone else as well.

"Girls do things together all the time," she said, spreading her arms wide for dramatic exasperation. "Honestly, it's never as straightforward as just calling one and hoping they come alone. Unless they are alone. But if they're not they'll be with someone else. Lauren was never alone when she went places. When I knew her, it was either me or Carly Storm."

Carly Storm! The name suddenly came back to her.

"I haven't thought about Carly in years," Luna said, but Beauséjour wasn't really paying attention. He had taken out a little book and seemed more interested in scribbling in it than listening to what Luna had to say.

"Bringing along someone for support," Beauséjour muttered.

"Hey, girls have been doing that way before it became fashionable to do it at meetings with the management! Are you even listening to me?" Luna finished in frustration, and Beauséjour looked up at her, slight surprise on his face.

"Of course."

"What are you doing?"

"Sudoku," he said, and turned the book around, to show her. Luna opened her mouth trying to create sound before finally getting somewhere.

"Why?"

"Patterns," Beauséjour said. "Sudoku helps me think about patterns. Sorting out the numbers, determining where each one goes. Sometimes it's easy, because you have enough of the number to determine where it will go in a certain sector, but sometimes you don't. Sometimes," and now he was warming to his theme, "it's the absence of other numbers that make it clear where a number is going to go." Luna looked at the Japanese puzzle, curious. "This sector needs a nine, but it's not clear where. Two spaces at the top could be nine, or…could they? The horizontal requires an eight and the vertical here needs a two, so nine is definitely not going in the top line. But if it doesn't, then it has to go on that line in *this* sector."

"But that wasn't what you were trying to achieve," she pointed out, and Beauséjour grinned at her.

"No, but sometimes you have to concentrate on the bigger picture when the details don't entirely match up."

"Oh," Luna said, starting to understand the point he was making.

"Ms Lora," Beauséjour suddenly said, and he stood up. Luna suppressed her own grin when she saw that she had been right – Dione Lora had brought Kendal Leigh with her, though Beauséjour didn't seem particularly put out by this. "I can appreciate this must be a hard time for you."

"It's the worst," she said, and she sounded weak, probably a side effect of having cried for goodness knows how long. If she was the killer, she was an incredible actor, Luna reflected. "Laura was my best friend. I mean we've been friends since high school. She was the most amazing thing to ever happen to me. I just can't believe she's gone." Even the other bridesmaid seemed to think this was slightly over the top, and she rolled her eyes a little, presumably hoping that no one would notice. Luna had to admit she was slightly surprised by this as well. She couldn't remember Lauren ever mentioning Dione Lora. If they were best friends, one member of the friendship was definitely giving a lot more to it than the other.

"Finding the body must have been awful for you," Beauséjour said.

"It was terrible. I just…I couldn't believe it…just seeing her sitting there dead." The other bridesmaid harrumphed slightly, and Beauséjour turned his attention to her.

"I'm so sorry, I've forgotten your name."

"Kendal Leigh," she said, reaching across to shake Beauséjour's hand, though with what was seeming to be typical rudeness, he ignored it and left Luna to shake. She was quite stunning, Luna reflected. Whereas Lauren had a kind of girl-next-door vibe to her, who caught the attention of those that liked that sort of naivety, and Dione was a mousey sort of woman who was clearly the donkey to Lauren's racehorse, Kendal was a step above both appearance wise. She had blonde hair which was tightly done up, with little curls floated around her face, full lips and very dark eyes, all of which made her much more captivating than either of the other two in the bridal party. Luna wondered what sort of person she was. She had often felt that beauty of that level on the outside was unlikely to be mirrored on the inside. Though maybe she was just being bitchy.

"You weren't at High School with Lauren, were you?" Luna asked.

"Oh no. I've only known her for the last few years. We met at a conference for animal welfare and became good friends." Beauséjour caught Luna's eyes and she gave an ever-so slight acknowledgement. Lauren Foster was quite the altruist.

"I'm assuming that you never left the Princess' side during the wedding?" Beauséjour asked her, and Kendal shook her head.

"Not really," she said. "I was with her during the wedding, of course; we both were. And we got ready together: me, Loz, Di and the maid, and then we went to the wedding and then we came here."

"You were with her when she got in the car?" Kendal was about to open her mouth, but this time Dione cut in.

"Not exactly. We got in the car and had to wait because there were a number of people that spoke to her before she got in." Luna nodded subconsciously as she remembered the woman with the hat meeting with the Princess outside.

"Who was the last person you saw talking to the Princess?" Beauséjour asked, and Dione frowned as she tried to remember.

"I don't really know," she said. "I was sort of on the far side of the car, so I couldn't really make out the faces of the people. Just the trousers, and everyone was really wearing black, so it could have been anyone."

"It wasn't anyone," Kendal corrected. "It was you." She levelled her gaze at Beauséjour and Luna looked at him in surprise.

"Interesting," Beauséjour murmured. "She went to the car immediately after talking to me?"

"That's right," Kendal agreed. For a moment Luna wanted to say something, to correct Dione when she mentioned only seeing trousers, and to correct both at them not mentioning the woman in purple, but she kept her peace. Let people talk themselves out of their alibi, Beauséjour had been known to say. Guilty people generally tend to want to confess to someone. Although, as another little detail came to mind, Luna wondered if perhaps there was something she could say that would get a response.

"Was the Princess upset when she got in the car?" Luna asked, and the two bridesmaids looked surprised.

"No, what makes you think that?" Dione asked.

"I thought I saw her have a disagreement with someone," Luna replied, hoping it was vague enough not to be pursued. She glanced across at Beauséjour, and was happy to see that he had decided simply to absorb the conversation rather than be part of it. She didn't particularly want to come under his scrutiny in front of the bridesmaids.

"Oh," Dione said vaguely.

"She was fine," Kendal said. "A little emotional, but this is…was her wedding day." Her voice trailed off a little when she changed the tense of the verb, and Luna noted that both women were shaken again. Surely, they weren't killers? They seemed to care way too much if they did.

Or maybe that was the point?

"Why did the Princess use the antechamber?" Beauséjour suddenly asked.

"The what?" Dione asked, puzzled.

"The waiting room. Changing room. Where she was murdered. Why did she use it? Why not just go straight to the wedding?"

"Oh, well you must have seen her new outfit. The red dress. She needed to get changed, and that was the place to do it." Dione said.

"Why did she want to get changed?" Beauséjour persisted.

"The wedding dress was cumbersome," Kendal replied. "I think she wanted to change into something easier to get around with. She had decided on red because of the red chrysanthemums. That's why she had the single one in her bouquet." Luna noticed Beauséjour frown slightly at this, but said nothing. Instead, he changed tack.

"Not her choice though," Dione said, and Beauséjour looked at her curiously. "The chrysanthemum. She didn't really like them, to be honest. Not her type of flower. But the groomsmen were sort of set on them."

"You didn't approach the body," Beauséjour asked her, and she looked at him.

"I told you I didn't," she snapped.

"No, no, I know, I know," he agreed. "It was too much," he added. "All the blood."

"There was no blood," Dione corrected him, and this time neither Beauséjour nor Luna could disguise their surprise.

"There clearly was," Luna said. "There clearly was heaps of it on the floor and someone had stepped in it."

"Oh, well, yes, that was odd," agreed Dione. "She bled out a lot while I went to get Dr Kilman." Luna opened her mouth to argue, but she felt Beauséjour's hand on her arm and went silent.

"I think that's probably about enough for now," Beauséjour said. "I'm sorry to have to put you through all that again, Ms Lora. And your help has been invaluable Ms Leigh. Thank you very much."

The two women nodded, and then stood up, walking out, the white of their dresses making them look like phantoms returning to whatever darkness they had come from. Before they got to the door, however, Beauséjour suddenly spoke up.

"Oh, sorry, one more thing, Ms Lora," he said, though both women turned back to him. "Was there a cup or a mug in the room when you first entered?"

"No," Dione said after a moment. "Not at all."

"Thank you," Beauséjour smiled at her. The two women looked unsettled, but then left for good. Luna followed them, closing the door behind them.

"What the actual?" she said.

"I can't believe she didn't see any blood," Inspector Kelinaw added, and Luna paused, having totally forgotten that the other woman was in the room.

"God, you're quiet," Luna said.

"I'm not supposed to be involved, remember?" Kelinaw said with a little smile. "So, I'm keeping my mouth shut, and my ears open."

"She was very definite about there being no blood," Beauséjour mused. Kelinaw gave an intake of breath, as though recalling something, and reached into her pocket to hand a piece of paper to Beauséjour, who thanked her.

"Why lie about something like that? Also, I don't think you were the last person to see the Princess before she left. I'm sure I saw her with someone else." Luna pouted, but Beauséjour didn't seem particularly put out about having been lied to.

"People only lie when they are covering up something they don't want to come out," Beauséjour said absently, reading the paper that Kelinaw had handed him. "Which begs the question, what is Kendal Leigh covering up?"

II

Axton Beauséjour, Luna Rochique and Inspector Dani Kelinaw stepped out of the makeshift interview room and paused as they surveyed the dining room in front of them. People were muttering among themselves, some were nibbling at the food, but many looked distracted and anxious.

Nervous? Luna looked at Beauséjour, but he didn't seem particularly concerned.

"What's the plan?" Kelinaw asked.

"Well, it might be an idea to talk to them all at once, while they are together. Get an idea of the sequence of events. We need a timeline, an order of visitations. Or attempted visitations at least." Beauséjour turned to his companions, who both nodded their agreement. With that he moved forward to the primary table, and rapped his cane sharply on it. This was met by a look of irritation from a number of people, particularly the bridal party seated there, and Luna was sure she saw one of the staff wince, making her wonder how expensive the table was that Beauséjour was now banging away at with blatant disregard for the cost.

"Sorry," Beauséjour started, "if I could just have your attention for a few moments. I had a question which I thought I'd pose to all of you."

"I thought you wanted to talk to us one on one, because it would be *better*?" Clayton Reese snapped out, his voice full of irritation.

"The way you approach an investigation can change all the time," Luna retorted, surprised at how defensive she sounded. Beauséjour may be a bastard, but he was her bastard, and no one but her was going to put him in his place.

"The thing is, I need to know who spoke to the Princess when she arrived here this evening," Beauséjour said. "I think I have an understanding of who saw her at the wedding, but between that and now, I'm not sure if anyone spoke to her, outside of her bridesmaids."

"And the maid," Kelinaw added, and Solomon Burton stood up, but Kelinaw held up her hands and took a step back.

"Well, I did," Clayton Reese announced, without any further prompting. "Me, and my wife, Blake. We're Lauren's godparents. We had to step in and tell her how proud we were of this day. So proud."

"And how proud her parents would be," Blake Reese added, and Luna was delighted she had guessed her identity correctly earlier. Blake stood up, and Luna guessed she was perhaps older than her appearance would have let on. "It's such an achievement. She's a marvellous person and has done so well."

"This should have been the best day of her life," Clayton Reese said.

"And now it's the last," Beauséjour intoned, and Luna cringed.

"Good grief man, don't you have any soul?" Reese roared at a volume that was presumably on behalf of everybody.

"Forgive me, Mr Reese," Beauséjour said, waving his hand and sending the mixed message that he didn't particularly want forgiveness. "Please sit down. Would anyone else care to admit they spoke with the Princess before she died?"

"My brother and I did," a woman said, and the room turned to look at the speaker. She was seated towards the head of one of the two perpendicular tables of guests, and was a striking woman with long dark hair, though there was a touch of steel about her features that made her slightly less attractive than she probably could have been. Lines at the corner of her mouth indicated that she often was unimpressed, and there was even the hint of permanent frown lines between her eyebrows. "As did the Count and Countess," she continued. "We all met with her to give her our congratulations on the day."

"As new family members would," Beauséjour agreed, and Luna realised that the speaker was presumably Prince Michael's sister, which meant his brother would be the other noble at the other table, but neither were part of the bridal party. Not unusual, but worth remembering.

"Exactly," agreed the younger prince – sitting at the other guest table in the same position as the female speaker. "We couldn't have been happier that she was joining the family."

"Princess Stephanie and Prince Lucas," Beauséjour whispered to Luna. "The younger siblings of Prince Michael."

"Oh," Luna nodded, but was again pleased she had picked the identities of the speakers correctly. They were quite different to their brother. Lucas was much younger, or at least seemed to be. If Prince Michael was in his forties, Prince Lucas seemed almost twenty years younger; his hair curly and sandy, and he had a moustache that must have been grown to make him look older, though it ended up looking surprisingly fake. Prince Lucas was very endearing, a little like a puppy dog, and Luna wondered if he was simply decadent to annoy his older siblings.

"At the risk of being rude, however," Beauséjour went on, "Count and Countess?"

"Countess Emília Vladen, my husband, Count Aleš," the older lady at the table with the princess spoke up. "The Princess was speaking generally, I should add. We all went and gave Lauren our congratulations, but we didn't go together. That would have been too many people. Far too silly."

Luna guessed that Countess Emília may have been the same age as Mrs Reese, but she didn't bother to hide it, unlike the latter. Countess Vladen's hair was steel grey, and she had an unforgiving face, with cold, diamond blue eyes. If a face could be described as no-nonsense, Countess Emília had that face. Her husband, on the other hand, seemed far more relaxed. Count Aleš was definitely more laid back than his on-edge wife, and was perhaps the only person who genuinely seemed relaxed in the room.

What was obvious was the fact that Princess Stephanie's table was presumably the prince's guests, while Prince Lucas' were the Princess' guests. As Luna studied the table layout, she realised the tables were designed to properly mirror the other. Countess Emília was sitting opposite Princess Stephanie, and Count Aleš was to the Countess' right. Clayton Reese, on the other hand, was opposite Prince Lucas, and Blake Reese was to his left.

"Of course it would," Beauséjour said, though it sounded like he didn't really care whether it would be silly or not. "So, just their royal highnesses and the Reese's? A surprisingly short list."

"I spoke to the Princess before she left for the reception," and Cameron Regan stood up, straightening his suit as he did. "Not when we got to the reception, however."

"I have you on the list, Mr Regan," Beauséjour said, and Regan looked as though he were about to say something, but opted instead to simply sit down. "Oh, of course, Beddows," Beauséjour said as an afterthought, and the butler turned to look at him. He wasn't seated at a table, rather he was standing towards the back of the room, waiting patiently.

"Indeed, sir," the man said haughtily.

"And the maid," Beauséjour muttered.

"Yes, sir," came a new voice, much to Luna's surprise. She scanned the direction of where it had come from, and saw the maid that the she and Dana had encountered earlier in the day. She seemed to be stressed, which she hadn't been earlier, though in fairness that could be said about anyone in the room. And no doubt someone was giving her a hard time for the Princess being murdered on her watch.

"We both served the Princess during the day, and spoke to her," Beddows said.

"Was she a good employer?"

"What sort of a question is that?" Prince Michael said, turning from his chair to Beauséjour, suddenly full of fire."

"One that tries to determine if there is motive to kill, Michael," Beauséjour replied evenly.

"How dare you," Michael almost snarled.

"Their Highnesses were the finest of employees and we were totally dedicated," Beddows said, quickly putting out any fires. "Is that not true, Birman?"

"Very, sir," she nodded.

"What's your name?" Luna suddenly asked.

"Birman," Beddows replied, and the professor shot him a look.

"She wasn't asking you, Mr Beddows. Your first name, Ms Birman," Beauséjour said.

"Amy," she replied, and gave Luna a small, grateful smile.

"Hopefully no one is lying," Beauséjour said with a cheerful grin, and Beddows glared at him. "This case should go swimmingly while everyone is telling the truth." With that he turned and headed back to the antechamber. The room behind him, however, was distinctly uncomfortable.

III

"I didn't speak to the Princess," Lord Pero Petar announced.

When Luna had approached him, he had taken a step backwards into the shadows, and was now mysteriously speaking from them, which was very disconcerting. Lord Pero Petar already had a dark appearance, with a goatee that looked as though he were trying to imitate the devil, and the gleam in his eye certainly didn't help. Axton Beauséjour had encouraged her to talk to him as they had returned to their interview room. He suspected that the groomsmen would be more inclined to open up to her, and though she was dubious as to his motives, she couldn't deny her own curiousity.

"So, you never made contact at all?"

"I knocked on her door after Hunter summoned me. I think I maybe even called out her name, but there was no response."

"Summoned you?" Luna wondered, surprised at the choice of word.

"I was sent to get the Princess because she was taking some time, but the door was locked and she didn't respond. I didn't want to disturb Prince Michael, so I went to get Lord Pero." Hunter was standing near Lord Pero, but more in the light, and Luna wondered if they realised how they were standing.

"When she didn't answer me, I summoned Prince Michael and Ms Lora," Lord Pero picked up. Luna wanted to see if Beauséjour was taking everything in, but at the same time didn't want to make it obvious that she was acting for him, or that he was just inside the antechamber, listening to the entire conversation.

"So, the door was locked when you both went to the Princess, and remained locked until…"

"Until Burton opened it for the Prince," Lord Pero finished. "Anything else you want to quiz us on?" He looked at her and Luna smiled back sweetly.

"No," she said. "No, that's about all. Thank you."

"Are you doing the investigation or is that professor?" Hunter Shelby asked. When he spoke, there was a weariness to him, and Luna realised he looked younger than he actually was. There was the possibility that he may very well be the same age as the Prince and Lord Pero, but actually didn't look it. She shrugged, hoping to come across as mysterious, but Shelby and Pero simply looked irritated and the conversation was now clearly over. Pero separated from the shadows and the pair went back to the bridal table, while and Luna entered the antechamber.

"I feel like we're in prison," she grumbled.

"Until we sort everything out, I can't let anyone leave," Inspector Kelinaw apologised. She didn't look enormously happy about the situation, but unlike them, she could leave at any point, Luna reflected. Solomon Burton was also in the room, his hands crossed, looking annoyed as always. Luna suspected he was tired of being left out of the loop, but at the same time, he was a suspect.

Though so was she.

"Did you have the only key to the corridor?" Beauséjour asked Burton, and the burly security man looked at him.

"There's a second," he replied.

"Where? With whom?"

"My understanding is the manager of the Royal Arms was holding onto it," Burton replied.

"Perhaps we should find out if that is still the case," Beauséjour mused.

"Did you have keys to building exit from that corridor?"

"No, but you're barking up the wrong tree. You should probably speak to some of the other staff that were guests," Burton added, and the other three in the room looked at him. "Barrera, for instance," Burton supplied.

"Barrera?"

"Zakaria Barrera. He's the head chef. Personal chef to the Prince. He was organising the meal tonight, but he's also a guest."

"What?" Luna asked, surprised.

"The Prince was grateful to the staff that have been by his side for so long. Myself, Barrera, Kilman." He shrugged as he came to the end of his list.

"Beddows?"

"Beddows wasn't a guest," snorted Burton. "He's the butler." Luna glanced at Beauséjour and he nodded slightly at her. There was certainly no love lost between Burton and Beddows.

"Let's go talk to Barrera," Beauséjour said to Luna, and she turned to leave the room with him.

"Shall we just wait, then?" Burton asked, annoyance in his voice.

"If you wouldn't mind," Beauséjour said, not looking back at him, which was probably for the best, Luna reflected. The look on Burton's face was murderous.

The two walked out of the antechamber, and Beauséjour pointed a towards another doorway, clearly heading towards it. Luna paused to actually take time and work out how many doors there were, realising she hadn't bothered until that point. The antechamber and egress they were heading to were on the wall behind the table of the princess' guests, while the corridor that led to the rest of the building and their crime scene was opposite them. The main entrance was the only other door, to their left.

"The murderer would have had to have come back through here, surely?" Luna suddenly said, stopping Beauséjour.

"Unless they went out a window." Luna opened her mouth, and the closed it again.

"So, the murderer might not even be here?"

"It's always a possibility," Beauséjour replied.

"But you don't think so?"

"I think," Beauséjour said, but before he could continue, someone was suddenly standing in front of them. She was a curious woman, possibly in her late forties, early fifties, with the air of someone who had just fallen into a hedge and pulled herself out again.

"Hello?" said Beauséjour.

"Oh, hello," the woman said, and Luna noticed she had an American accent. She was in the process of correcting her glasses, as well as seemingly trying to stabilise herself. Truth to tell, Luna thought she could smell the aroma of alcohol coming from her. "I'm Borna Vanja," she continued, and Luna thought she could hear the slightest slurring of her words. "I just wanted to say," and she paused to straighten her hat, "that I never spoke to the Princess tonight."

"At the reception?" Beauséjour said.

"No, never. Ever." She looked at him myopically, and then straightened her glasses, which had somehow managed to become crooked again. "I never spoke to her, and I didn't murder her." Luna wondered if she had lost her mind.

"Well, thank you for that," Beauséjour replied cautiously.

"I mean, just to be clear," Borna said.

"Right," Beauséjour nodded. Borna gave a nod in return, and then turned and walked away, but looked back briefly and they both nodded at each other. Luna watched her go and then turned back to her former mentor.

"What was that about?" she asked incredulously.

"Beddows, Birman, Burton, Barrera, Borna," Beauséjour listed. "Beauséjour," he concluded.

"What?"

"I'm just thinking that maybe you were absolutely right about the 'R' being a 'B'," he reflected.

"It doesn't exactly narrow it down, does it?"

"No," Beauséjour agreed. "It doesn't narrow it down at all." He let the sentence hang in the air for a moment, before setting off again towards the entrance to the kitchens. Luna paused, replaying the conversation over in her head. She suspected she was missing something significant, but she couldn't immediately tell what it was.

Chapter Six

A Cornucopia Of Clues

The Royal Arms, Reidon

I

If they knew better, some might assume, based on the activity in the kitchen, that a murder hadn't taken place, least of all the bride of the function that was being held. The aroma of the food was incredible, with the scent of each dish mixing with the others to create a mouthwatering perfume, dominated by paprika. The smell of stock, infused with cumin, wafted from giant pots coming to the boil on impressive ovens that were clearly designed with feeding an army in mind.

Chefs darted back and forth, cooking filet mignon (with…was that a balsamic glaze?) and French onion chicken, preparing green salads and panzanella, and plating up what was being sent to them. Commanding them all like some sort of pirate captain, was Zakaria Barrera; a man who was seemingly dressed to give that very impression. He had a three-quarter length black jacket, secured by gleaming gold buttons, and cuffs that were turned up and trimmed, also in gold. There was a ruffled white shirt beneath, with a stylish white cravat, and of course Barrera himself, with his huge eyebrows and massive beard. The only thing missing was the eyepatch, Luna reflected, suppressing a giggle.

"Main course is supposed to go out in seven minutes," Barrera roared, and his voice was tinged with a Greek accent. "I have a reputation to uphold no matter what may have befallen the guests. The meals of Zakaria Barrera will go down as a feast for those that may not be long for this world!"

"Ouch," muttered Luna to Beauséjour, who nodded. Even he thought that was a little on the nose.

"What do you two want?" Barrera bellowed, though it was an unnecessary attempt to get above the noise in the kitchen, as it wasn't that loud they couldn't hear his voice from about a metre away.

"I'm Axton Beauséjour, this is Luna Rochique," Beauséjour began. "We've been asked to look into the murder of Princess Lauren. We had some questions for you if that was OK."

"For me?" Barrera asked, incredulously.

"You seem surprised," Beauséjour replied.

"I didn't kill her," Barrera said, and his voice suggested that should have been the end of the conversation.

"You'd be surprised how many guilty people say that," Beauséjour offered. "You might also have seen something regardless of your guilt," he continued, cutting off Barrera's outrage.

"Why would I have seen anything?" Barrera quizzed.

"Mr Barrera, at the risk of sounding cliched, we're the ones here to ask the questions. If you keep asking us, it defeats the purpose," Beauséjour replied, a touch of annoyance in his voice.

"It was a rhetorical question," Barrera replied, and tugged his beard. "I didn't see anything. It was to have been a wonderful night. A night that everyone could be proud of." There was something in his voice, but Luna was sure it was regret rather than sadness (and definitely not guilt). Clearly the only thing Barrera seemed remotely interested in was his food.

"I'm sure that you'll still get a five-star review for this meal," Luna drawled, and a fire lit up in Barrera's eyes.

"Oh, you think my concerns are petty?" he demanded, as his voice reached 12. "You think that I have nothing better to do than wait around to make sure that everyone else's lives are sorted out, and put mine on hold."

"Do you have somewhere to be?" Beauséjour wondered, curiously.

"I," and the chef threw his hands to the sky before reorientating, "have other things that I could be doing. All of the meals are going to be late, because of the ridiculous police."

"To be fair, I think they have policies they need to proceed with," Beauséjour offered reasonably.

"Well, I have policies that I need to proceed with," Barrera said, unnecessarily dramatically.

"Did you meet with the Princess after she came to the reception?" Beauséjour snapped, bored with the conversation and losing his temper a little.

"Yes, I did," the chef replied, his eyes rolling. "Of course I did. We're great friends. And I consult with her about the menu."

"Not the Prince?"

"The Prince I have served for years. He has implicit trust in me. No matter what I serve before him, he would eat it. Would he like it? Of course, because there is nothing Zakaria Barrera makes that is not succulent. Would he have heard of it? Perhaps not, but he would still eat it because the Prince is aware that Zakaria Barrera is a gourmand, and as such knows what is tasty and what is not. The end." He turned his gaze toward them imperiously, and for a moment Luna got the impression that he was indeed at the prow of his galleon, looking down at them on the docks.

Then she decided he was just bigger than her and louder.

Do your stuff, Professor.

"So, to be clear, the Princess did not trust you implicitly?" Barrera glared at Beauséjour and looked ready to blow a gasket.

"Of course she did!" he exploded. "I said we were great friends, did I not?"

"Yes, but you also said you didn't need to consult with the Prince because he trusted you implicitly, but you were consulting with the Princess, which suggests that in fact, she did not."

"Masri!" he bellowed, and there was a moment where everyone paused. Finally, a tall woman sauntered over to them. Like everyone else, she was dressed in kitchen whites, but unlike everyone else she had an air about her that suggested she wasn't going to be disturbed by her boss' behaviour.

"Yes, chef?"

"Tehmia Masri. My Chef de cuisine," Barrera announced. "Explain. Why I meet with the Princess."

"Oh," she said, and a wry smile appeared on her face, as though she were amused at some inside joke. "Princess Lauren likes to be involved with the menu. She feels it is important. Also, she has some allergies, and so she likes to make sure we remember to accommodate them."

"Liked," Beauséjour corrected.

"Sorry?" Masri queried.

"Liked. Liked, felt, was, had, remembered…past tense."

"Oh yeah, of course," Masri nodded. "Well, she liked to make sure we knew."

"You were likely to forget?" Beauséjour wondered.

"Of course not," Barrera replied, though he was calmer now. "I remember everyone's eating habits. The Princess' allergies, the Countess being a vegetarian, the Count requiring a specific diet to accommodate his diabetes. These are all things that Chef Executif does not forget."

"Or Chef de cuisine," Masri added.

"Did you notice anything about the Princess when you visited her?" Beauséjour continued, focussing back on Barrera.

"No," Barrera shrugged. "I passed the Countess coming out as I was about to go in. I explained the menu to the Princess. Of course she adored it. Everyone was very happy, there was delight and wonder at how Zakaria Barrera could create such treats, and that was the end of it." There was a pause as the four stood awkwardly. "Well? Can I return to the reception?" Barrera demanded.

"I wasn't stopping you," Beauséjour pointed out.

"Wait, you're going to the reception?" Luna asked.

"That is where the guests of a reception go," Barrera replied sharply.

"So, you're a guest as well as the chief executive?"

"Chef Executif," Barrera spelt out. "And yes, I am both of those things. My loyalty to the Prince would never go unrewarded. I am an old family friend. When he is King, I shall remain by his side as his personal chef."

"Thank you," smiled Beauséjour, and stood back, gesturing to the door. Barrera glared at him, and then at Masri, and then turned to storm out of the room. "And thank you," Beauséjour added to Masri, who smiled in return. Beauséjour turned to follow Barrera out of the room, but Luna paused.

"He seems a lot," she said.

"Chef?" Masri clarified. "Uh, well, yeah. He's very proud of having climbed from kitchen hand to chef executif of a royal household. I suppose if I was in his position I might feel the same." She shrugged, and Luna pulled a face.

"He also seems to have a temper," Luna added.

"Oh yeah, that's true," agreed Masri. "Don't they say all great artists do?"

"You're not a great artist?"

"I put a very distinct line between being a chef and being an artist," Masri laughed. "You're an artist, I'm a chef. I'm happy for the two not to overlap. Chef? Well, he sees it differently."

"Right," Luna nodded. She turned to walk out, giving Masri a slight nod on the way.

II

They were back in the Princess' changing room, though thankfully the body had been taken away. Inspector Kelinaw had assured them that nothing else had been touched, though Axton Beauséjour had made some points about the newer footprints in the blood on the floor, and Kelinaw looked uncomfortable. The smell in here was nothing like that of the kitchen. Luna wrinkled her nose as the odour of blood refused to settle in the background.

"We couldn't get her out without disturbing some things," said Kelinaw. "We tried our very best not to disturb anything else."

"Why have we come back here?" Luna asked, trying not to wretch.

"Death," Beauséjour said, and Luna looked at him. "That's the smell. It's not pleasant, but it lingers."

"You don't have to keep pointing out that she's dead, you know," Luna retorted.

"What do you mean?"

"When that chef...Masri...you had to point out she was using the wrong tense because Lauren's dead. You seem to want to hammer the point home. I sometimes wonder about your social skills," she grumbled.

"People like to smooth over awkwardness," Beauséjour replied. "I don't like it. I don't like pretending bad things haven't happened. You can't sweep things under the carpet. You have to…" He paused, frowning. "I don't like this." He said, and Luna looked at him, confused.

"This?"

"*This*," he emphasized. He waved his arms around, swinging his cane in the process and narrowly missing a variety of furnishings. "This room is… There're things here that don't make sense. Those gloves," he said.

"Yeah?"

"Why are they here? Why are they here and the murder weapon isn't?" He swung around, jabbing at the chair on which the Princess had been found, with his cane. "Why waste time writing an initial on the mirror instead of calling for help? Why…" He paused again, getting swallowed up by thought before restarting. "If she was writing a B, and she died, wouldn't she have slumped forward?" He briefly mimed drawing and then expiring, leaning forward.

"So, it was an R," Luna said. "She finished it and slumped back, out of energy."

"Did she?" Beauséjour muttered. "A B in the mirror. A footprint in blood. A pair of blood-stained gloves." Again, he paused, and again, Luna watched Axton Beauséjour fall into his own thoughts. He suddenly turned and looked around the room, his eyes searching something out, but what it was she had no idea. "Interesting," he murmured, and Luna forced herself not to fall into the trap of asking him what he was talking about. She had come to the conclusion she was obviously the sidekick, but she wasn't going to be stereotypical about it. Inspector Kelinaw, however, was more traditional.

"What's interesting?" she asked, and Luna smirked, glad she wasn't the one who did it.

"There's no knife. But there's a small red petal." Kelinaw looked at Luna, and Luna simply smiled, realising that Beauséjour had just decided not to answer the question.

"Can we go through her clutch?" Luna asked Kelinaw. The inspector fished into her own bag and then handed over a pair of latex gloves, which Luna put on. The clutch was now sitting in the chair that had once been occupied by its owner, and Luna opened it. Beauséjour turned to Kelinaw, and Kelinaw handed over latex gloves to him, but he moved around the room slightly so he could get access to the drawers in the dressing table that the Princess had been seated at.

"Professor, there are two notes in here," Luna said, and Beauséjour looked up at her.

"What do they say?"

"Well, one says, *L – As much as it hurts me, I understand why you are going through with this marriage. I'm not stupid. That doesn't diminish my love for you. I hope that there will still be a place for me in your life once this is over.*" Luna looked at the note, then handed it to Beauséjour who studied it for a moment.

"Looks like a man's writing," he said. "Not that that's proof of anything."

"The other one is only part of a letter, I think. It looks ripped. But you can make out *You don't want to cross me.*" Luna handed that over as well, Beauséjour glanced at it and then handed them both to Kelinaw.

"Signed CR," Beauséjour noted as Kelinaw took them.

"Looks like it was an R," Luna said, a little annoyed at being proved wrong. Kelinaw studied the two letters thoughtfully.

"The CR one is typed," the inspector said, and Beauséjour nodded approvingly. "The other one looks like it was written in more of a hurry." She produced some sealable bags and slid the notes into them. Beauséjour, meanwhile, reached into the drawer that he had opened and held up the item that he had found. It was clearly a Tarot card, with a woman on it, holding a goblet in each hand.

"Does that mean something?" Luna wondered.

"Well, it's odd that the Princess would have it in her dresser drawer on her wedding day," Beauséjour said. "It's the Queen of Cups."

"Compassionate and caring," Luna said. "The Princess?" Beauséjour opened his mouth to say something, but then closed it, and moved across the room, handing the card to Luna on the way.

"Professor?"

"Carpet," he said. He knelt down to the edge of the rug that was in the room, now blood soaked and sticky, and lifted the edge up slightly. Carefully he pulled something out from underneath it, and held it up.

"Is that a hair pin?" Inspector Kelinaw asked, curiously.

"I think so," Beauséjour replied. "And it looks very expensive." He handed it over to the two women, who both looked at it thoughtfully. It seemed to be made out of ivory, but there was a skull carved into it, giving it a fairly grim mood.

"If Burton gives us permission to move forward, we'll test the gloves for DNA," Kelinaw said.

"I wouldn't bother," Beauséjour replied. "I don't think you'll get anything from them. They're very neatly folded. So much so that they clearly haven't been used today."

"Oh, they're from stock somewhere," Luna suddenly realised. "For the waiters."

"Exactly. Someone's playing games with us. Someone's trying to make sure we look in the wrong direction. I think it's time to meet with the players and ask them a few pertinent questions," grinned Beauséjour.

PART THREE

NOTHING BUT THE TRUTH

Chapter One

Playing The Cards That Are Dealt

The Royal Arms, Reidon

No one was happy.

Not in the sad way. Some were not sad, but were also not happy. Luna Rochique thought that was interesting. She wanted to say something to Beauséjour, but the prince had offered him the groom's chair, and Beauséjour had taken it, consequently sitting on a throne of sorts and looking as though he were secretly enjoying it. Which might explain why Lord Pero Petar looked unhappy, as he had moved from his chair to the right of the Prince, and was now sitting awkwardly on a guest's chair rather randomly in the middle of the room. Beauséjour had a casual lack of respect for anything formal, which amused Luna, who shared his view, if she were honest.

As he surveyed the crowd, they looked nervous and awkward. A small group of people hoping for a nice dinner to celebrate a wedding, now all suspects in the murder of the bride. Trapped in a building until a decision was made by bureaucrats. On a list of the most uncomfortable situations to be in, this had to be close to the top, no matter how good the food.

Lord Pero's decision to move away had resulted in the entire bridal party doing the same, and so Hunter Shelby was now pacing around the end of the bridal table, looking less like a caged lion and more like a bored domestic cat. Dione and Kendal had both set up chairs near the table that the bride's guests were seated at. Prince Michael's siblings were still seated at opposite tables; the young Prince, Lucas, on the bride's side, while Princess Stephanie was on the groom's.

There was definitely a similarity to them, Luna decided, with all three having the same aquiline features, though youth made the younger Prince more accessible, while the dark features of the Princess gave her a haunting beauty.

Luna thought there was a certain irony to the idea that the room seemed to be split into two teams. Clearly it had been intentional, but was there actually a genuine competition going on? She had managed to acquire a piece of paper and a pen, and sat down beside Beauséjour, where she began drawing a rough sketch of the room. In her own mind she was keen to put the players of their little drama into place. Having never met them before she was determined to keep track of the players.

There were some people she was able to identify without too much difficulty. The Reeses were easily identified; Clayton (the godfather!) in his charcoal grey suit, his more flamboyant wife, Blake, seated beside him, and both near the head of their table, close to Prince Lucas. Though if she were honest, Luna had to admit she hadn't seen the three interact terribly much.

On the opposite table, Count and Countess Vladan in their darker suits, sat with Princess Stephanie. She knew Cameron Regan, with his blue suit and pencil moustache, seated at the Princess' table as well. The three staff members of the Prince – Dr Kilman, Solomon Burton and chef executif Barrera, were all at the Prince's table. The slightly odd Borna Vanja was at the Prince's table as well. She and Dr Kilman seemed to be as thick as thieves, chatting to each other, occasionally laughing at something, which earned them a glare from at least one other guest. Then there were two women at the Princess' table who she couldn't really place. They definitely hadn't met with Beauséjour yet, so she didn't feel entirely guilty about now knowing their names. And of course, standing ever present at the ends of either table were Beddows, the butler, and Amy the maid. Beddows looked slightly bored, Amy, more interested in studying her feet.

Luna went back to studying the two mystery women, who both looked strangely out of place. One was the woman in the purple dress and amazing hat who had perhaps made Lauren cry when they met before getting in the car. She was calm, a point of stillness in a room of tension, and on top of that was quite striking. Luna couldn't shake the feeling that they had met before somewhere, the feeling of familiarity hitting her every time she looked at the woman. Maybe she simply had one of those face. She drew a question mark at the woman's position on the table, and then when she remembered the fact this was the last person Lauren spoke to before leaving the church, she underlined it.

Then there was the second lady, who was probably in her early forties, but looked haphazard and somewhat *thrown together*. She had a hat on her head which had a strange floral bouquet that the lady seemed intent on fighting with, and there was a nervous energy about her, as though she was on the verge of being caught with the silver in her purse. Why might someone be nervous at a wedding, Luna wondered, though if the bride had been murdered it wasn't really that big a mystery, was it? And yet, this woman was so nervous, if she was the murderer, Luna suspected Kelinaw and Burton could simply wait an hour and the woman would confess.

"Before Mr Barrera's beautiful meals are brought out," Beauséjour said, and the room went dead silent, hanging on his every word. There hadn't been much conversation before, but as the blanket of hush descended on the room, Luna shivered at the obvious change. "I should like to ask you all some questions. I feel that there are some people here who have perhaps been moderate with the truth." He surveyed the room, and Luna watched as individuals met his challenge, or flinched and couldn't make eye contact.

With a flourish, Beauséjour pulled out the red petal that he had found in the room, and Luna watched as a brief flash of annoyance crossed the Inspector's face.

"We found this in the late Princess' chambers. I think it's pretty obvious where it came from." He paused, and Luna saw Lord Pero and Hunter shuffle in their places.

"But I didn't go into the room. I didn't see her," Pero said.

"Did Mr Shelby go with you when you went to fetch the Princess?" Beauséjour asked.

"No, I stayed with the Prince," Hunter said.

"But I didn't go in," Lord Pero reiterated. Suddenly, Beauséjour was up and out of the throne, walking around the table to confront the best man.

"Is there anyone who can verify that?" he demanded, and there was a new energy about him. Gone was the laissez-faire professor, now replaced by the bulldog prosecutor. Luna had remembered seeing this change in lectures. For the most part, Beauséjour had come across as a bohemian who didn't follow rules or formalities. But when he had properly decided to show them his lawyer side, he became a different person. There was a force behind him, released from some hidden safe. Suddenly he cared for no one, *except* the rules and formalities. Social conventions he had little time for. The criminal justice system? That was sacrosanct. "No? Mr Burton?"

When Beauséjour swung around to glare at the security guard, it was with a force that Burton recoiled from.

"I know Lord Pero went down alone, but I didn't go with him," Burton said, immediately throwing the best man under the bus.

"Why would I kill her?" protested Pero.

"Perhaps you should tell us?" Beauséjour said pointedly. Lord Pero looked at him for a moment, and Luna wondered if he was trying to work out what the right thing to say to Beauséjour was.

"I have no reason to kill her," he finally opted for, though Beauséjour was clearly not finished with his train of thought.

"Maybe Mr Shelby went into the room, stabbed the Princess, came out and locked the door, and then went to Lord Pero, thereby setting up an alibi?" Beauséjour gripped his cane and threw a look at Hunter Shelby.

"No!" the younger man exclaimed.

"No?"

"I would never kill her! I…" Shelby paused and everyone waited to see what was going to come out of his mouth. "I would never kill her," he finished lamely, but Luna doubted there was a single person in the room who wasn't drawing a different conclusion. Certainly, Prince Lucas seemed to be drawing the same conclusion, as the anger on his face was quite clear.

"Interesting," Beauséjour said, making it clear he had also reached that conclusion. "Because there was a shoeprint in the blood around the Princess. It was a man's shoe, not a woman's."

"It wasn't me!" Hunter protested.

"Or me!" Lord Pero quickly followed up.

"Well, there were definitely other males in the room," Beauséjour pointed out. "Mr Reese?"

"She was alive when I talked to her!" Reese snapped. "People talked to her after me," he added, a small note of triumph in his voice.

"And the same goes for my husband!" Countess Vladen quickly announced, and Count Vladen gave a small smile, before obviously realising how inappropriate it was, and settled back in his seat again.

"And me!" Barrera was the last one to alibi himself, but Beauséjour simply watched the three dispassionately. Finally, he spoke.

"So quick to defend yourselves. Though, I wonder Mr Burton…did you see everyone go down to meet the Princess?" There was another pregnant pause as Beauséjour studied Burton. The security guard looked uncomfortable, but finally responded.

"I did."

"No one saw her without you seeing her first?" Beauséjour clarified.

"That's correct." Burton held Beauséjour's gaze, to his credit.

"Interesting," Beauséjour muttered. He began to move around the room, a little like a shark circling its prey. Luna couldn't help but feel the analogy might have been closer than it should have been. "Perhaps the shoeprint isn't a clue," Beauséjour finally said. "Perhaps the shoeprint belongs to the Prince."

"It's not possible," the Prince said.

"Why?"

"I didn't go near the body, remember. I couldn't bring myself to," he continued.

"It's true," Dione spoke up. Mouse didn't just describe her appearance, Luna reflected, it was a fairly accurate summation of her personality as well. There was no doubting that the greyhound had passed but the donkey wasn't speeding up.

"Oh yes," Beauséjour murmured. "Not the Prince. But his name doesn't start with B." Around the room, people exchanged awkward looks, wondering what the comment was in reference to, before Beauséjour finally spoke again. "The Princess had scrawled a R on the mirror. In blood." He paused to watch the reactions, before continuing. "Or maybe it was going to be a B, but she couldn't finish it." Again, a pause to drink in their reactions. Rather unexpectedly, he suddenly grinned. "Well, that doesn't narrow it down, really, does it? Mr Barrera?

Mr Burton? Ms Reese? Ms Blake Reese? Any B's I missed?"

"My first name is Borna, but I didn't kill the Princess." Beauséjour turned to look at Borna Vanja, his eyebrows knitting in puzzlement.

"We know," Beauséjour said.

"I just wanted to be up front," Borna smiled apologetically. Beauséjour's frown deepened, but he refrained from making a comment. Luna suppressed a giggle, and wondered if Borna Vanya was trying to be helpful or simply being irreverent.

"I'm not afraid to admit my name also begins with a B," Beddows crisp voice rang out across the room. "As is Birman's," he added, indicating the maid beside him. She nodded her head a little, her curly hair bobbing slightly.

"We forgot you when we were going through the people who visited the late Princess," Beauséjour said amiably, and there was a look of shock on Beddows face, which was quickly replaced by the professional butler exterior. Nonetheless, Luna decided, Beddows was clearly riled, despite how well he managed to keep it off his face.

"The Princess was alive when she called upon me to get her drink. Again, others attended her after me." The two men looked at each other from across the room, and Luna was intrigued that the butler should be the man who clearly challenged Beauséjour more than any other.

"Fascinating," Beauséjour said, but there was a wicked grin on his face.

"Hardly, sir. It's my job," Beddows replied pointedly, but Beauséjour's grin didn't falter.

"No, Beddows," he replied, "it's fascinating that…" Beauséjour suddenly paused and then said "Forgive me. It's just my warped sense of humour." The grin never faltered, and Luna wondered what could possibly be going through professor's head. She wasn't the only one, as Lord Pero suddenly decided to speak as well.

"You find the murder of the Princess funny?" The man's dark features looked even more saturnine than earlier, and Luna wondered if he was attempting to turn the guests against the professor. The truth was, they weren't acting in any official capacity. Should the room turn, they simply wouldn't help, no matter how much Prince Michael might ask them to. For reasons she wasn't quite sure about,

Luna felt the need to defend her former lecturer.

"I think Axton looks at the world in a peculiar way," she said. Pero glared at her, but she held her ground, refusing to be intimidated by a Lord.

"That's very true," Beauséjour agreed, though Luna felt he wasn't helping things. He turned away, leaning slightly on his cane, his back to the crowd. Luna, however, could see everything he was doing, and she watched as he reached into the inside pocket of his jacket and withdrew the hairpin that he had found earlier. "That's very specific," he said, almost to himself. Beauséjour turned and held the hairpin in front of him, making it clear to everyone. "I wonder who this belongs to."

"It's mine." Everyone in the room turned to Princess Stephanie. She hadn't moved from her chair, and hadn't even really spoken loudly, but her voice carried across the room, and there was a quality to it that commanded attention. Princess Stephanie glanced up, her dark eyes matching Beauséjour's grey ones. "Before you say anything," she added. There was the hint of an accent to her voice, stronger than Prince Michael's but still decidedly not like the rest of the country. Luna tried to remember what people had said about Stephanie's upbringing, as it seemed her accent had been dulled to a more neutral European tone. She suspected that Prince Lucas would be in a similar situation to the rest of his family.

"You're wearing one," Beauséjour pointed out, but the Princess didn't miss a beat.

"It's a matching set. It must have fallen out."

"Countess Vladen has one as well," Beauséjour said, and Luna looked at the Countess. Sure enough, in her hair, she saw a similar clip to the one in Beauséjour's hand, the skull motif prominent.

"They are gifts to all women in the royal family," the Countess said. Like the Princess she had a commanding voice, and Luna wondered if they were directly related.

"Interesting," Beauséjour said.

"Is that all you're ever going to say," snapped Clayton Reese from the other table. Beauséjour turned to him, and Luna guessed that the older man was barely keeping his temper in check. He liked to be in control, she guessed, and didn't respond well to situations where he was put onto the back foot and made to do as he was told.

"You don't think it's interesting that every female member of the Crovanian Royal family got these and either Princess Stephanie got two, unlike Countess Vladen, or Countess Vladen has also lost her second one, just like the Princess?" Beauséjour's eyes bore into Reese's who backed down. "I find that interesting," the professor continued, and Luna glanced at Princess Stephanie who looked livid. Countess Vladen had gone red in the face. Neither of them had expected their lie to be called out, Luna guessed.

"Where there any other clues?" Beauséjour said softly. Nobody spoke, and Luna suddenly realised that he had been waiting for her.

"The letters," she blurted out, and as quiet as the room had been before, now it seemed like all sound had been sucked out completely. Were they all holding their breaths? It was fanciful, but it certainly felt that way. On cue, Inspector Kelinaw was bringing the letters out in their sealed bags.

"L," Luna began, "As much as it hurts me, I understand why you are going through with this marriage. I'm not stupid. That doesn't diminish my love for you. I hope that there will still be a place for me in your life once this is over." She looked up upon finishing, and noticed that people were exchanging glances with each other.

"Int…" Beauséjour began, but then stopped. "Sorry, Mr Reese. Shall we say curious instead?" He looked around the room, and Luna's stomach lurched. As much faith as she had in Beauséjour, the truth was she wasn't entirely certain he wouldn't say something that would throw her under the bus. It certainly wouldn't be the first time.

Oh god, did she have PTSD?

"Before we go on, before Axton decides to use it against me…to be clear, I once had a brief fling with the Princess." Luna looked directly at Beauséjour, who seemed a trifle hurt. In spite of that, however, his next words were still business.

"So that's why you were invited." Luna wondered if Beauséjour was playing up to the crowd, lulling them into thinking he wasn't going to dig into their pasts next. Using her as bait yet again. She set her jaw.

"Yes. That's why I was invited. She was in a band ages ago. We performed together. Then …we spent some time together." She couldn't quite keep the anger out of her voice, but Beauséjour didn't seem to notice.

"But you didn't write the letter." It wasn't a question, but Luna felt compelled to reply anyway.

"God no. That was years ago. I mean, she's lovely, but…" Luna let the sentence hang in the air.

"But you are a butterfly," Beauséjour finished. Luna opened her mouth to retort, but then brought her temper back into line.

"Harsh, but true," she admitted. Her lifestyle didn't really invite commitment, but it was an excuse, really. Luna herself didn't particularly want to get tied down to anyone. She had her own interests, her own passions and the opportunity to pursue both. She wasn't at that point in her life where she wanted to share it, let alone give it up for someone. She vaguely remembered Beauséjour describing her as a butterfly years ago. His memory was clearly as good as his attention to detail, she reflected, a little sourly.

"It wasn't the only letter," Beauséjour said, moving on without ceremony. "There was another. Or at least part of another one. A typed letter."

"You don't want to cross me. CR," Luna read out.

"Well now, Mr Reese," Beauséjour said, and the grin flickered across his face. "That *is* interesting."

"We treated that girl like a daughter when her parents passed away!" Blake Reese was almost out of her chair in anger, and even Beauséjour seemed surprised at her venom.

"Why would I even threaten her?" Clayton Reese asked, standing and putting his hand on his wife's arm. Beauséjour stared at him as though he were about to give an answer, and then abruptly changed his mind.

"This gets deeper and deeper," he finally said, turning away from the couple. "So many clues, so many people to point the finger at." Beauséjour had started moving away from the Reeses, and though it initially seemed casual, his next sentence was delivered to the person he had found himself beside. "Isn't that right, Mr Regan?"

Cameron Regan didn't even bother to look towards the professor. Instead, he reached forward and took the cup in front of him, taking a small sip, before speaking.

"Yes, my initials are CR, but I didn't kill her." He took another sip before deigning to turn back to Beauséjour. "I didn't even see her at the reception."

"You spoke to her before she left the church!" There was a sudden silence around the room as everyone wondered who had spoken. Luna saw that Beauséjour had turned to the back of the room, and the look on Beddows face made it clear who had spoken, even if she didn't now have her head lowered. Amy Birman, the loyal maid had been the one to speak up.

"Yes, alright, girl," snapped Regan, and Luna wondered if he was more annoyed he had been caught out, or if it was because Amy had been the one to do so. "I did. But she was alive when she got here, so I could hardly have been the person who stabbed her."

Beauséjour had seemingly lost interest in Regan, and was wandering around the room as Regan continued his justification, looking bored. Once again, Luna couldn't discern a specific destination but she was almost positive it wasn't random, though this time when he spoke it wasn't to the person he was standing near; in point of fact, he had found himself by the wall near the main entrance.

"It's all very interesting," he said, though it could have been to himself. "And there's a noticeable absence of the most important clue. No sign of the knife. Actually…" But this train of thought went nowhere. For a moment he stared at the closed door, and then he swung around, moving across the room, surprisingly swiftly for a man with a limp. "Tell me, Ms Lora, was there a glass in the room?"

"You asked me that before," Dione said, surprised.

"Yes," Beauséjour agreed, "I'm asking in case your memory has adjusted."

"No, I didn't see one. I distinctly remember."

"Your highness?" Beauséjour swung towards Prince Michael.

"Did I see a glass?" Beauséjour simply looked at Michael, and the Prince spoke again. "I…no, I don't recall one."

"Mr Burton," Beauséjour turned to the security guard. "Are you sure you saw everyone who went to the Princess?"

"Absolutely," Burton nodded.

"So, you're saying Mr Beddows didn't take a drink to the Princess?" Before the implications of Beauséjour's question could sink in, Beddows was already speaking.

"I most certainly did!"

"But I didn't…" Burton started, though Beddows cut him off quickly.

"Perhaps you were asleep, Mr Burton?"

"How dare you!" Burton rose out of his chair, but Beauséjour's cane flashed out, resting on the man's shoulder and firmly pushing him back in his chair.

"It's not important, gentlemen," Beauséjour said. "What is important is that the glass was missing. No knife, no glass."

"How is that important?" Another new speaker; Dr Kilman, who had remained remarkably quiet throughout, Luna mused. Given he was the one who examined the body, you'd think he'd have more to say. "She was stabbed."

Beauséjour turned to him, but his eyes didn't quite meet Kilman's, rather they glanced at someone else. Luna wondered what he was looking at and what he had seen.

"Stabbed? Yes, so she was. Repeatedly," Beauséjour agreed. "How much have you had to drink tonight, Dr Kilman?" Kilman turned red before their eyes, his blood rising in fury, though the entire room couldn't have failed to see that there were several glasses on the table in front of him.

"What the hell sort of a question is that?" he tried to shout, though his voice was a squeak. Prince Michael had put his head in his hands, a little embarrassed.

"It's a party," Beauséjour said reasonably. "You're a guest. Presumably you indulged?"

"Yes," Kilman blustered, the glasses in front of him already answering the question.

"So, you're happy to stake your professional reputation on the cause of death as stabbing?" Kilman looked as though he were about to deliver another angry retort, when clearly his brain caught up with him.

"I," he started, before changing tack. "Well, I mean, there should be an autopsy to confirm."

"So that's a no?" Beauséjour asked, and Luna could see the inappropriate grin dancing across his face.

"I will not be treated," Kilman began, but Beauséjour simply held up his hand.

"Calm down, Doctor," he said, "Let's assume you're right." Kilman may not have calmed down, but he did quieten down, though he still clearly seemed annoyed at the use of the word *assume*. "After all, there was the pair of white gloves, covered in blood. Evidence that would suggest you did your job well, Dr Kilman." This seemed to satisfy the Doctor, but Kendal gave voice to the room.

"You think they were the gloves worn by the killer?"

"East to get," Beauséjour offered. "There are plenty of waiters around who would have been wearing them. Mr Beddows would have a set or two. Come here, grab the gloves, grab a knife, go and stab the Princess. Then take the gloves off and throw away the knife."

"And not leave any evidence," Zakaria Barrera said sombrely.

"Except the gloves. Which the police have taken and will examine for DNA evidence," Beauséjour said. Having made his way to the front of the room he rested against the bridal table.

"But you said they could have been a waiter's. So, there could be other DNA on them," Barrera argued.

"Absolutely, which is not particularly useful," Beauséjour agreed. "But at least it proves Dr Kilman knows what he's talking about." There was a lull, and Luna wondered if the murderer was feeling confident with the events that were taking place, or if they were getting nervous. For the first time, it hit her that the murderer was indeed in the room with them. At one of the tables, there was a person who had decided to take the life of an individual and was now able to bareface lie to everyone else, devoid of the emotion one would expect from having taken a life. The idea of killing seemed so inhuman that Luna wondered how anyone could have done it and then gone to the reception to sit down and have dinner.

Whoever it was must have been a complete sociopath.

Axton Beauséjour stood up from his resting position, and put his free hand on his jacket, reacting somewhat in surprise. He reached into his pocket and pulled out a card – the card he had found in the drawer.

"Oh," he feigned, and Luna fought not to roll her eyes. "There's one more clue. A Tarot card. Specifically, the Queen of Cups. I wonder whose that might be." He looked around the room before saying "It's probably best to come forth before you're exposed." There was an edge of steel to his voice. From the bride's table, the woman who had been fighting with the fruit on her hat stood up, adjusting her glasses and looking ridiculously awkward.

"It's mine," she announced, looking around, nodding. She was still ridiculously nervous, and fidgeting a lot. "I'm Madame Jindra Pét'a," she said grandly, before giving a small bow, which resulted in her dropping her bag.

"You've remained very quiet all night, Madame," Beauséjour said pointedly, heading over to her to pick up the bag.

"I have nothing to say," Madame Jindra said, affecting an air of nonchalance. Luna watched Beauséjour slide the few things that had fallen out of the bag back in, including two Tarot cards. As he stood up, he held up the two cards.

"I wonder," Beauséjour mused, "if the Queen of Cups was deliberately placed upside down. Because you know what that means, right, Madame Pét'a?" Beauséjour paused as he handed the bag back, fixing Madame Jindra with a steely stare. "A deceitful, perverse woman. A liar and a cheat."

"Oh no that's not me at all," Madame Jindra protested.

"What do you do?" Beauséjour demanded.

"I'm a medium," Jindra said.

"And why are you here?" Beauséjour continued.

"I…I used to do readings for the Princess," Madame Jindra explained.

"And she invited you to the reception?" Beauséjour asked incredulously.

"Of course," Jindra said with a winning smile.

"And you visited her?"

"I…well," Jindra said, but Beauséjour scowled.

"Well done, Mr Burton," he said sourly.

"Indeed," Beddows said, his mask of professionalism falling a little. Solomon Burton was already spluttering, but Beauséjour simply held up his hand, dismissing Burton's incompetence. Luna noticed a small exchange of looks between Lord Pero and Prince Michael and guessed that Burton would be lucky to keep his job after this evening.

"Well, I did visit her, but only to tell her that she was going to die," Madame Jindra said, and there were gasps around the room. Even Beauséjour turned back to her in surprise. "Well, I knew, you see. I knew that she was going to die. I mean, the truth is I wasn't really on the guest list, but I had done a reading and in that reading the poor dear was clearly not going to make it. I had to let her know!"

"I knew you weren't a guest," Princess Stephanie suddenly scowled.

"Oh yes, and I saw you and I saw you," she pointed to both Stephanie and then Prince Lucas in turn, "meeting with the Princess. You were very upset," she said, staring at Prince Lucas. "I don't know why. But you, you were very upset."

Luna looked around the room, taking in the faces of everyone. Most seemed baffled, puzzled by this new information imparted by someone who seemed completely insane. But Prince Michael didn't. He actually seemed angry. Luna's thoughts were interrupted by Beauséjour who had taken control of the room once more.

"So, we've learned it wasn't impossible to get past Mr Burton to see the Princess. And we've learned that there is at least one liar among us who doesn't wish to be found out." Beauséjour handed back the Tarot cards to Madame Jindra, as he let his sentence sink in. Burton looked as though he wanted to defend himself, but was clearly struggling to find the words to do so.

"At least one," Luna emphasized.

"Indeed," Beauséjour agreed. "Interesting, wouldn't you agree Mr Reese?" Reese glared at Beauséjour but said nothing. Before anything else could be said, the doors to the kitchen swung open, and waiters entered, bearing meals. Barrera seemed to have lost interest in what was going on and turned to try the dish he had concocted. "I propose that we eat our meals," Beauséjour said.

"And then?" Luna asked.

"And then, we should have a séance."

Chapter Two

A Trio of Tales

The Royal Arms, Reidon

I

The guests were starting to get claustrophobic. The Royal Arms was a relatively big building, but when you couldn't leave it, trapped within by a police force who, ironically, couldn't enter, it all became so much smaller. Patience was not endless, and for some, there was a genuine concern that they would never get out.

Luna Rochique suspected Madame Jindra Pét'a was one of those that was worried this might be the end of the line. She had taken it upon herself to enter the antechamber where Axton Beauséjour had held his private interviews, and was pacing the room.

"Do you have something to be afraid of?" Luna asked, and Madame Jindra's head snapped around to look at the new arrival. It was the most precise move Luna had ever seen the woman make. Almost as soon as she had, though, the fruit on her head seemed to slide, and Madame Jindra was again trying to reset it so it looked normal and in place.

"Well, *probably*," she said, and Luna raised an eyebrow. "Well, we all have something to hide, don't we?" She adjusted her glasses and also the shawl that she was wearing. For the first time Luna was able to look at the woman's garb properly, and realised that it was slightly extraordinary for a Royal Function. Though dark and austere, with flashes of navy blue, moss and juniper, it still looked a little like a carnival fortune teller's. Add a turban and you'd have just the right amount of racism for the seventies. With the hat, however, Madame Jindra looked less like she was trying to culturally appropriate, and more like she was a hippy. "You'll tell your boyfriend I'll need that card for the séance, by the way," Jindra added.

"He's not my boyfriend," Luna scowled. "He's old enough to be my dad!"

"Oh, I don't judge, dear," Jindra said, waving a hand dismissively. "No, if you're both happy, that's all that matters. That, and if he can get the wee one up when you need a good seeing to, eh?" She gave a wink that she probably thought was conspiratorial, but Luna now felt made her seem like she had lost her mind.

"Thanks for the analysis, but no, that still doesn't change the fact he's not my boyfriend," Luna said. "I'll tell him you need the card, but who exactly are you going to get in touch with?"

"Oh, it was his idea for the séance, dear," Jindra protested. "I will hold it, but I have no idea who I'll get in touch with. I assume he hopes that we'll be able to get in touch with Lauren, poor thing. She might still be here. There are certainly presences in the building that haven't moved on yet." Jindra looked around, as though the presences were waiting to have a quick word there and then.

Oddly enough, had Madame Jindra known Luna Rochique any better, she would have known that Luna was one of the more receptive people to speak to. Luna had a fervent passion for the supernatural, which penetrated a lot of her music videos, and occupied a great deal of her spare time. On this occasion, however, Luna had no doubt in her mind that Jindra was a fraud. She was far too put together to be anything other than a charlatan.

"Well, let's hope that Lauren can point us in the right direction and tell us who the killer is," Luna said, fighting to not roll her eyes.

"I certainly hope so," Jindra agreed. "And if she can't, then maybe one of the others can tell us something that they've seen. After all, a kiss from a succubus can have more import than we think." Luna paused and then turned back to Jindra.

"What did you say?"

"Maybe one of the others…"

"After that," snapped Luna.

"Oh, uhm, ah, a kiss from a succubus can have more…"

"What the hell does that mean?" Luna glared at her.

"Oh, I'm not sure," Jindra said. "It was a phrase whispered to me by one of the voices here." She waved her hand airily around the room, suggesting that there was a whole host of spirits lining up to give her information. "Does it mean anything?"

"No," Luna replied, and then stormed out. Inside the antechamber, Jindra gave a soft smile to herself. Outside, Luna frowned, disturbed at how shaken she had been. She hadn't sung *Kiss from a Succubus* since the night she and Lauren had gotten hot and heavy. It was an awful piece, and she wanted to cast it aside, particularly as she got more and more successful. How could Jindra possibly have known about that song?

II

"It concerns me about how long this entire process is taking," Prince Michael muttered, though the urgency in his voice was clear. With his siblings to one side, and his groomsmen on the other, he looked like the leader of a pack of wolf hounds ready to hunt something to eat. Standing before them in the corridor that they had chosen, the diminutive form of Inspector Danielle Kelinaw hardly seemed like any opposition whatsoever to the might of the Royal Family of Crovania.

And yet, Kelinaw remained unperturbed. She stood there, taking the verbal assault from the Prince without batting an eyelid, and remaining calm the entire time. In some ways it was clear that her unflappability was annoying some members of the entourage more than the fact they were cooped up inside the barracks.

Michael had led them to the access corridor that gave entrance to the various side rooms, including, of course, the room that now remained out of bounds to everyone; not that anyone had any desire to go into it, having reached a point where it was clearly giving off the smell of stale blood.

"If I might remind you, your Highness," Kelinaw said, "this wasn't my idea. This was Mr. Burton's. I was happy to investigate the murder as a proper police investigation, which would have meant we interviewed you and then sent you on your way. Or maybe even the other way round. All this would have been cordoned off and everything would have been done exactly the way it should be done. But *your* security chief was the one who insisted that his people trumped mine, and you appeared to support him."

"In fairness, I said I wasn't sure," the Prince said.

"The Prince has the right to make any decision he likes and that is the end of it," Lord Pero enforced.

"Of course, and I don't object," Kelinaw said, even daring to smile.

"But I can't do anything if decisions are made that tie my hands. And you have entrusted the investigation of this murder to a man who I know nothing about and who I am expected to trust absolutely. I'm doing my best under fairly difficult circumstances." She looked at the group, challenging each and every one of them. Both Hunter Shelby and the younger Prince Lucas shrugged, accepting what she said. Lord Pero clearly didn't, but on the other hand, wasn't really able to challenge her. She was, fundamentally correct, and even though he didn't like it, he had to admit she was right.

There was one person, however, who seemed at odds with the general consensus. Princess Stephanie, in her dark burgundy dress, had already quite the impression on Kelinaw, and the inspector wasn't quite sure how to deal with her. Now, Stephanie's eyes flashed and she turned to her older brother with clear irritation.

"Why don't you just let Burton do his job and dismiss these people and that strange man in the beret?" she demanded. When she became angry, her accent got thicker, and as such was now stronger than both her brothers.

"We must be seen to be impartial," Prince Michael replied calmly, but still seemingly crushing any further discussion. Princess Stephanie wasn't so easily ignored, though, and both the princes inwardly groaned when she began speaking again, years of familiarity leading both men to know what their sister was going to be like now.

"We are the Royal Family," she said. "We are above reproach! And we stand by each other at all times."

"Do we indeed?" Prince Michael said, and for a moment there was a pause. Inspector Kelinaw couldn't help but notice Prince Lucas flinch at the comment, and wondered exactly what was going on between them. "Regardless of this situation, this is my wife we're talking about, and her death should be investigated. I will not have anything interfere in finding the culprit, least of all some petty squabble over who exactly is responsible for the investigation!"

"We shouldn't be here if she was alive when we left her," Prince Lucas suddenly said. "Force that professor to talk to the Reeses. They're the ones who have something to hide."

"They aren't the only ones, brother," Michael said, and again Kelinaw saw the steely undercurrent between them.

"There was nothing going on between me and Lauren," Lucas snapped. "You need to let it go, for the love of God."

"I know what I saw, Lucas," Michael snapped back.

"Enough," Princess Stephanie said, interrupting the fight. "Have you forgotten where you are and who you are? And if you are so concerned about mad flings, maybe you should have been concerned about mine!"

"I'm sorry, what did you say?" Inspector Kelinaw said, and the three royals looked at each other. Nonetheless, they remained silent. "Princess Stephanie?"

"My understanding is that I'm not obligated to answer your questions, or Mr. Burton's," she said haughtily. "I only have to abide to that idiot in the scarf." With that, she turned and stormed up the corridor, back to the main reception hall. The remaining men glanced awkwardly at each other, before turning to Inspector Kelinaw.

"She's correct, of course," Prince Michael said, though it came across as an apology, and Kelinaw nodded gracefully. "She has the utmost respect for the police."

"Or course she does," Kelinaw said. "And she should, your Highness. After all, regardless of who is doing the questioning and having the discussions, the person who arrests the murderer will still be me."

III

Axton Beauséjour pushed the large, wooden door that led to the reception hall open, and stepped into the room that provided a lobby of sorts from the front entrance. He briefly ran a hand over the rather elaborate chiselled lion that was on the door, musing on how the main entrance itself was the set of doors, plain and featureless. Step through them and you step from the common world to the upper class, with all the trappings that go with it.

Standing in the lobby, looking out through the windows, was the mysterious woman in the violet dress and matching hat. Beauséjour peered through the matching window on the opposite side of the main entrance and saw the police outside. He counted four of the white vehicles with the Crovanian coat of arms on their front doors, the blue and red lights on the top flashing and causing the lobby itself to flip between a world that was either underwater, or potentially hell.

The lady didn't pay attention to Beauséjour when he entered, and he wondered briefly if she had noticed him. He coughed slightly to get her attention, but she didn't flinch. Beauséjour was immediately aware that she was putting on a performance. It was a useful tell.

"I don't think we've been introduced," Beauséjour said.

"You know we haven't," the woman murmured in response.

"Well, you know who I am. You are?" There was a pause, and Beauséjour wondered if the woman would deign to give a response. She seemed to be thinking along the same lines, but finally opted to turn to him. She looked to be about the same age as the late Princess Lauren, Beauséjour thought, but had to admit he was terrible with guessing people's ages. She was tanned and blonde, with her make-up looking rather perfect. Her eyebrows were perfectly sculpted, her lipstick applied to give full and well-shaped lips. She wasn't a model, Beauséjour guessed, but she was something else that required a close attention to appearance. An influencer, perhaps?

"Lady Jacinta Daniels," came the response. She didn't offer her hand, which was fine as Beauséjour had not moved his hands from his cane.

"Lady?" he queried.

"Correct," she responded. Her accent was neutral, Beauséjour thought. Wherever she had come from, she had worked hard to remove drawls and uncommon inflections to speak English in such a way that hid any trace of a birth location.

"May I ask where you gained your title?"

"I was born with it," she replied.

"I said where," Beauséjour rejoined, his tone non-committal, but he was clearly not backing down from the line of questioning.

"Crovania," Lady Jacinta said, as though she thought Beauséjour an idiot. In court, there had been times when a prosecutor's witness had given an answer that Beauséjour hadn't been expecting, and he had learnt to not give away his surprise in that situation. Old habits refusing to die, Beauséjour's face remained neutral when she gave her answer, but all the same, the professor was thrown a little by the response.

"You're a member of the Royal family?" he asked, keeping his voice level.

"A cousin. Not close, to be clear," she added. "But all the same, there is a precedent for us coming to receptions."

"A tradition?"

"If you like. The Prince and Princess didn't want a huge reception, as you know," – this last part was delivered almost as though she were trying to catch Beauséjour out, which he found interesting – "but there were still some family members that were allowed to attend if they were keen."

"And you were keen?" Beauséjour mused.

"Not really," Lady Jacinta admitted. "But my parents were unable to come and I was. So, I did the good daughter thing and came in their place. I figured they would be proud of me, and I would get some brownie points." She looked Beauséjour in the eye, challenging him to disagree with any part of her statement.

Beauséjour said nothing for almost two full cycles of the room flicking between scarlet and cobalt.

"So, I'm assuming you don't know the late Princess particularly well," he finally said.

"No, sadly. I never met her at all," Lady Jacinta said.

"You didn't speak to her after she arrived here?"

"No, I didn't feel it was my place. I assumed Prince Michael would introduce me."

"Your cousin," Beauséjour said, unnecessarily.

"Indeed," Lady Jacinta replied, and there was a barb in her voice again. Beauséjour's comments were not being missed, and she was happy to make it clear.

"Do you know your cousin very well?"

"No," Lady Jacinta said without prevarication. "He probably doesn't remember me," she continued. "He's a bit older than me."

"Yes, I suppose by the time you were born he was a teenager," Beauséjour mused. "Not really fun for either of you to hang with."

"Well, you don't really hang with the crown prince and heir apparent of the Royal Family."

"I'm sorry this day has turned out the way it has," Beauséjour offered, and he was a little surprise to see a crack appear in the façade.

"It's not your fault," Lady Jacinta said softly, and this time her emotions seemed real. Beauséjour cocked his head slightly, about to say something, but then decided better of it. She still presented something of an enigma, he reflected. For the moment he decided he didn't want to make that enigma difficult to deal with.

"Thank you," he finally opted for.

IV

When Beauséjour stepped back into the reception hall, he was surprised to find Luna waiting for him.

"I thought you might have come this way," she said, enthusiastically.

"You did?"

"Well, someone said they thought you had gone through the door," she shrugged. Before he could continue, Luna grabbed him and pulled him away from the tables at the centre of the room. The problem with a hall like this, she reflected, was that there was very little space to have private conversations, unless you wanted to actively leave the room, in which case you may as well announce that you were planning on having a secret meeting. "I've just been chatting to Madame Jindra Peta," she started.

"Pét'a," Beauséjour corrected.

"Whatever," Luna growled. "She can't be the real deal, can she?" He looked at her in surprise.

"I thought you of all people would be able to tell a charlatan," Beauséjour said.

"She knew the song that Lauren and I sung all those years ago. Like the exact title," Luna said, and realised she was gabbling slightly.

"It can't be that obscure," Beauséjour said.

"I've never sung it since that night. I mean, it's really bad." She grimaced slightly at the memory of it. "You know what thing where you think you're really cool, and then ten years later you look back and realise you have no understanding of what cool is, and being pretentious really isn't it, and also, lyrics aren't clever just because you're using slightly obscure words in them."

"I'll take your word for that," grinned Beauséjour.

"She's weirded me out," Luna grumbled. "And she thought we were dating."

"Us?" Beauséjour said in surprise. "Me dating you?"

"Excuse you," Luna snapped. "I'm extremely eligible. You'd be lucky to date me."

"I wasn't trying to be offensive, just," he shrugged.

"I know," Luna said. She was surprisingly unsettled and sensitive, she realised. Had Madame Jindra's words really had that strong an effect? It seemed so unlikely.

"I just met Lady Jacinta Daniels," Beauséjour said, and Luna snapped back to reality.

"Oh, the unnamed guest," Luna nodded.

"Indeed. Not that it was much help," he added. "There were some odd things. Apparently, she's a relative of the Prince, which begs the question why was she sitting on the Princess' side of the room. And she's oddly casual for a royal. Even a lesser one. But she has never met the Princess so it's probably not that important."

"That's not true," Luna said. Beauséjour gave her a look, and she continued. "I saw her. I recognised her because of that hat. She definitely spoke with the Princess. I saw her."

"It's odd how many people are determined to lie to us," Beauséjour muttered. "Weddings always manage to bring up some sort of dirt from the past, don't they?"

Chapter Three

Trying to Establish Order

The Royal Arms, Reidon

I

"Would it be an imposition," Axton Beauséjour started, but was quickly interrupted. He and Luna were back in the antechamber, along with the dedicated Inspector Kelinaw, and it was to the latter that Beauséjour was talking to, though the former was who interrupted.

"He means it would be," Luna drawled, to which Beauséjour simply raised an eyebrow before continuing.

"Would it be an imposition for you to ask Mr and Mrs Reese to join us in here, please, Inspector?"

"Not at all," Inspector Kelinaw replied. "I'm just a butler after all." There was an awkward pause, before the Inspector laughed heartily. "I'm joking. I'm quite enjoying being the tea girl. All of the glory, none of the hard work. If you solve this, it'll give me a very easy day." She strolled out, still chuckling to herself.

"She is weird," muttered Luna.

"People are people," Beauséjour shrugged. "Sometimes people even call me weird."

"No," Luna mocked. "You? Incredible." But Beauséjour has already moved on from this train of thought.

"What was the order of people who saw the Princess after she got here? It's not straightforward. By the time Shelby got there, the door was locked, so Pero didn't enter, and then the Prince and Dione had to get Burton to open the door."

"Do you think we should ask them to serve our dinner here?" Luna wondered, as she caught a whiff of the aroma wafting out of the kitchen next door.

"Yes, we should. Who was first? What did Lucas say?"

"Lucas?"

"Prince Lucas, Prince Michael's younger brother."

"Oh, uhm, he went but not at the same time as his sister, who didn't go at the same time as, uhm…" Luna struggled for a moment, patting at herself trying to work out where she had put her piece of paper with the seating plan on.

"The Count and Countess Vladen," Beauséjour supplied.

"But separately? Wait, Madame Jindra said she saw the Prince and Princess – one was leaving, one was arriving"

"The Reeses fit in their somewhere, as does the Count and Countess," Beauséjour added. He was looking around the small antechamber as though he wanted a whiteboard to draw on.

"I suppose Madame Jindra is having her meal," Luna mused.

"She was here?"

"Yes. Plus, we're not out there eating," Luna said pointedly.

"Go and get our meals," Beauséjour suggested. Luna shrugged for a moment and then stood up from the chair to exit, but was interrupted by the entry of Mr and Mrs Reese. They were, she decided, the most American people she had met in a long time. Quite aside from their accents, there was something quintessentially US about them and she couldn't quite put her finger on what it was. Perhaps it was simply an arrogance, as they walked in with the sense that they were already at home; an entitlement that possibly came from wealth rather than origin. After all, there were plenty of nice Americans around.

"You wanted to see us?" Blake Reese said, and though it was amiable, there was an edge to her tone of voice.

"In the middle of our meals, which we are struggling with anyway, given the circumstances." Given the chance to examine him up close, Luna realised Clayton Reese's stony-faced, grey-haired visage reminded her of Clint Eastwood, in a slightly less cool way. Truthfully, he looked more like a gangster than a cowboy, but maybe an older Dirty Harry.

"You said that you saw the Princess," Beauséjour cut quickly to the chase. "I was wondering when."

"What do you mean? I didn't check the time," Clayton Reese snapped. Blake Reese had sat down on one of the comfortable chairs in the room (and for the first time, Luna appreciated the fact that the chairs were very plush armchairs, and she wondered if this was some sort of room where people retired to after dinner to smoke – it was old fashioned, but it might make sense), though when Inspector Kelinaw indicated to Clayton Reese he should do the same, the man angrily shook his head.

"I suppose it couldn't have been too long after she arrived," Blake Reese mused, far more controlled than her husband. Luna had originally thought that Mrs Reese was perhaps a newer wife, given that she seemed, at first glance, a lot younger than her husband, but now they were face to face for the first time, she realised she had misjudged them. Mrs Reese was probably only a few years younger than her husband, but thanks to some hair dye, a little make up and perhaps just taking better care of herself, Blake Reese simply gave the impression she was much younger than her husband.

She was also clearly the voice of reason between the two. It didn't take a genius to work out that Clayton Reese had an explosive temper and was probably prone to losing control at the slightest sign of things going off the rails. His wife, however, was more likely to rein it back in again, and bring the best out of her husband. They were a good partnership, Luna suspected.

"You saw them arrive?"

"No, but we arrived when the maid was leaving with the bouquet. I presume she was taking it somewhere to be preserved as a memento," Blake Reese said.

"You both like her, of course," Beauséjour said.

"The maid?" Clayton Reese asked, perplexed.

"The Princess." Beauséjour's voice was measured, but Luna could sense the annoyance.

"We loved her," Clayton boomed, trying to keep control. "Adored her, in fact. That's why it couldn't have been me who wrote that ridiculous letter. She was like a daughter to us. When her father died, I made it my mission to make sure she had a father figure in her life. She never had to worry."

"Did you like the Princess, Mrs Reese?"

"Yes, she was delightful. I mean, obviously we were of different generations," and suddenly Luna saw an older woman despairing of the youth of today. It was so cliched it almost made her laugh. "I really do think she should have worn a veil. It was a bit tacky not doing that. Also, that red flower in the bouquet was a bit odd. When you're having a white wedding, you don't do that." She wrinkled her nose slightly, and Luna couldn't help but smirk, though she turned to Beauséjour when she did to avoid it being seen. To her surprise, she saw Beauséjour frowning and wondered what was bothering him. If anything, Blake Reese was quite growing on her, rather than being an irritant.

"What did you say to the Princess?"

"We wished her the best, of course," Clayton barked. "She was quite tired, to be honest. A little exhausted. I suppose she was overwhelmed with the big day."

"She didn't say much, you mean?"

"No, not really," Clayton looked to his wife, who nodded her assent. "We did most of the talking. She just said thank you, or the like. Then we left. There were other people who wanted to see her."

"Lining up outside, you mean?" Beauséjour asked curiously.

"Oh, uhm, that young Prince," Reese said, looking to his wife.

"Prince Lucas," she supplied.

"Yes, he was coming as we were going."

"Did you see Mr Burton?" Beauséjour wondered.

"The security man?" Reese clarified. "Well, uhm, I think he was at the door to the corridor, maybe?"

"We definitely saw him at some point," Mrs Reese added. "I'm not sure if it was then. But it was at some point."

"Thank you," Beauséjour smiled. "I think that's all."

"For now, you mean," Reese grumbled.

"Yes, if you like," Beauséjour agreed, but Clayton Reese just looked sour and stomped out of the room. Mrs Reese opened her mouth as though she were going to say something, but then clearly decided she wasn't going to. Instead, she smiled and followed her husband out. Luna wondered if she was going to apologise for or defend her husband.

"So, the Reeses, Prince Lucas, Madame Jindra, Princess Stephanie…" Beauséjour started.

"Zakaria Berrara as well at some point, remember," Luna added, and Beauséjour nodded.

"Well, it's a start."

"The start," Luna grumbled. "Of a very long list."

II

"Did you mean to bring in the older couples at the same time?" Luna asked, as she dug into her meal. With the Reeses having left, she had taken the opportunity to get both her and the professor's meals. At the same time, Kelinaw had gone to summon the Count and Countess Vladan.

"I hadn't considered it," Beauséjour said absently. Kelinaw entered the room, followed by the older Royals. As Kelinaw sat down, Beauséjour slid his meal across to her and she gave a grateful smile and started to eat, surprised at how hungry she was. Both the Count and Countess sat down opposite the trio though, they were comfortably a decade or so older than the Reeses. They also couldn't be more different. Luna almost thought that as American as the Reeses had looked, the Vladans couldn't have looked more European. Both in dark outfits, both very formal, both very austere. Count Aleš Vladan seemed very frail, his skin pale and the dark veins clearly showing on his hands and neck. His white hair was thinning, and his cheeks and eyes were sunken. Yet despite the fact he looked as though he might slip away at any moment, there was a glint in his eye; a cheekiness that suggested a humour kept well hidden. For the first time, Luna thought that she had met someone that she might genuinely like.

She hoped he wasn't the killer. That would be disappointing.

Countess Emília, on the other hand, was much less warm. Not as old as her husband, she nonetheless was lined and white, her dark eyes glaring above a beak of a nose that made her look like some albino bird of prey.

"I was wondering," Beauséjour started, "if you could possibly tell us when you saw the Princess. Not necessarily the timing as it were, but more who you followed and so forth."

"Well," drawled the Countess (and she spoke as though she had a plum in her mouth), "it was after Stephanie. Lucas and Stephanie had told us they were going, but obviously we take a lot longer to get anywhere." The Count gave a weak smile, acknowledging this.

"You saw Princess Stephanie leave?"

"Oh yes," the Countess said, and it became very clear that she had appointed herself speaker on behalf of both of them. "She was leaving as we were going down the corridor."

"That chef chappie came after us, if it helps," the Count said, and his wife shot a look at him.

"The Reeses, Lucas, Jindra, Stephanie, the Count and Countess and Zakaria," Inspector Kelinaw said, pausing in her dining to confirm the order.

"Did you see Mr Burton as you were coming or going?" Beauséjour wondered.

"Oh, I don't recollect," the Countess sniffed. "We aren't here to keep tabs on the staff."

"He was a guest as well, wasn't he?" Beauséjour pointed out.

"Probably. I did say to Michael that I thought it was foolish that he was dining with the help. Sends the wrong sort of message, to be honest."

"Yes, I can imagine it does," Beauséjour murmured, clearly not interested in this line of the conversation. "Can I ask, do you have any idea of who might want to kill the Princess?" There was a pause from everyone around the room at this question. Luna was surprised to hear Beauséjour come out with it, not least because he hadn't posed it to anyone else, which made her wonder why he was so interested in what the Vladans opinion might have been. The Vladans, on the other hand, seemed uncertain as to what to say.

"I wouldn't have thought anyone would want to kill the young thing," the Count finally said.

"Please Aleš," the Countess said, looking at him. "Murder is an unpleasant thing Professor...what did you say your name was?"

"Beauséjour."

"Professor Bowsayjoor," the Countess said, but was interrupted.

"Beauséjour."

"Professor," the Countess scowled, "the people who were invited to the wedding are not the sort to commit murder. Only the very best sort is here. People above reproach."

"Murder is an amazing leveller, Countess Emília," Beauséjour replied. "Passion and a lack of control can affect everyone, regardless of wealth and class. It doesn't matter who you are or where you're from, you can still be small enough to want to solve your problem by destroying it."

"Unnecessarily graphic, Professor," the Countess said haughtily.

"I apologise," Beauséjour replied, though there didn't seem a lot of honesty in the statement, and slightly less care. "What did you and the Princess speak about?"

"We just welcomed her to the family, officially," the Countess replied airily. "It wasn't a long conversation."

"Princess Lauren didn't have much to talk to you about?" The Countess shot a look at Beauséjour, before deciding maybe the question was inoffensive.

"No, she didn't say much at all really. I think she was a little overcome." The Countess paused for a moment, waiting for Beauséjour to add something, but when he didn't, she stood up, her long black dress swirling around her, and her husband took his cue, pulling himself out of his own chair with no small amount of effort. Extending an elbow, the Countess turned to leave, her husband dutifully taking the extremity and shuffling as quickly as he could.

"Countess, just one small thing," Beauséjour added. He reached into his pocket and pulled out the small evidence bag that contained the silver hairpin with the skull on it, looking moodily back at them. "You said this was a gift to all females in the royal family."

"That's correct," the Countess said, inclining her head.

"How many did you each get?"

"Just the one," the Countess continued. "They are hand crafted by Prince Michael's great grandmother and handed down through the family. There aren't that many, so the highest-ranking female royals are given them.'"

"And Lauren was becoming one of those," Beauséjour muttered.

"Precisely. If that's all?" Beauséjour gestured that he had nothing more to say, and the pair left.

"Why would Stephanie lie about something she could so easily be caught out in?" Luna wondered.

"She was caught off guard," Beauséjour answered. "She's hiding something, so she lied because it was the easiest thing to do. But in doing so, she inadvertently drew attention to herself. They're all being very polite, not dumping anyone else in the cooking pot. They need to be seen as supportive and caring, because that sort of person would definitely not be a killer. Even the innocent ones are playing a part now."

III

"Do you think this wedding is odd?" Beauséjour suddenly asked. They trio had been quiet for a while, though Luna had to admit she wasn't sure why. It was like when you were a kid and you had to have a minute's silence and think about the people who had surrendered their lives for their country, but as a kid, you just sat there thinking "I wonder how long a minute is". Luna suspected she was *supposed* to be thinking about something important, but the truth was, she didn't know what that was. Now, however, she had been given some direction.

"I've never been to a wedding like this before, but I don't know if that's odd, as such, because, I don't really move in these circles," Luna admitted.

"I try not to understand the upper class. It's all too odd for me," Kelinaw added. Beauséjour seemed lost in his own thoughts, before turning to the Inspector.

"Did someone say something about Prince Michael needing to get married?"

"Oh," Kelinaw mused. "I don't remember, if I'm honest," she said, "but it's sort of true. Tradition dictates that you have to be married to be crowned king. I don't know why, really." She shrugged, before continuing the train of thought. "We have a lot of silly traditions, but that is true. I do wonder why he chose Princess Lauren, though. I feel as though there was something that went on with the younger Prince and the Princess."

"And Lauren?" Luna said, surprised.

"That's the impression I was getting," Kelinaw affirmed.

"Not the only ones, either," Beauséjour mused.

"Oh come on, that was years ago," protested Luna.

"I didn't mean you," Beauséjour said, not registering her indignation. "Something Hunter Shelby said. Or didn't say, more accurately. He was about to say something then censored himself. And then there's Cameron Regan."

"What about him?"

"He was at the Bride's table, so presumably he was her guest. Although..." Beauséjour trailed off, and Luna scowled.

"Will you focus?"

"I am focussed!"

"On the conversation, then," she snapped.

"Regan was the Princess' guest, but what was their connection?" Inspector Kelinaw let out a long sigh, and Beauséjour and Luna turned to her.

"I assume you want me to go and get Regan?"

"Oh, that's kind of you to offer," Beauséjour smiled genially. With exaggerated effort, Kelinaw dragged herself out of her chair and left the room.

"So, you think there were a few ex-lovers in the room?" Luna asked, her curiosity roused.

"I think," Beauséjour started, and then paused. "I think," he said, picking up again, "that neither Michael nor Lauren have necessarily gone into this marriage for the sake of love."

"You're not a romantic, are you? Should make you very happy," Luna pouted.

"You're not a romantic, either, Ms Rochique," Beauséjour said pointedly, and she grinned at him.

"I sort of like the idea of romance," she said.

"I quite like the idea of being old with someone who knows you better than anyone else," Beauséjour said quietly. Luna's eyebrows raised.

"Really?" she said.

"Well, old age, I suspect, is possibly a lonely and scary place. It'd be nice to know someone was holding your hand as you walked that particular path." Luna studied him thoughtfully.

"Every so often I feel I have completely misjudged you," she said, and there was a small smile on her lips. Beauséjour was about to say something, when the door opened, and Kelinaw strolled back in, followed by the saturnine Cameron Regan. He sat down in the chair opposite the table, managing to look as though there was no thought in his movement, and yet remaining extremely cool in the process.

"Why were you invited to the wedding?" Beauséjour asked without preamble.

"I'm a friend of the bride and groom," Regan replied, equally to the point.

"In what capacity, Mr Regan?" Beauséjour pressed, and Regan regarded him before answering.

"I'm a business rival to the Prince," he said. Beauséjour simply raised an eyebrow, and Regan seemed to accept it was hardly a good answer. "The Prince and I are both in real estate. I'm big in the US, he's big over in Europe. We're about to enter the UK market, but obviously there's not really a great deal of room for us both, so it's a tight squeeze. We don't always see eye to eye."

"So, the Prince thought, *I'll just invite my worst enemy*, and that was all good?" Beauséjour couldn't have delivered the question more scathingly, but Regan took it in his stride.

"It's not a hate-filled relationship," Regan shrugged. "Frenemies, if you like." Luna suddenly remembered their first meeting, and the odd comment he had made.

"When I asked you whose side you were on, you said definitely not Prince Michael's," Luna said. "You did not make it sound like you were frenemies." Regan looked at her, and then gave her a wolfish grin.

"Very good, Ms Rochique," he said. "That is true. Maybe I'm underplaying our rivalry just a little."

"And your relationship with Lauren?" Luna held his gaze and for the first time Regan shifted a little uncomfortably.

"Yes, I suppose," he grudgingly admitted.

"So good friends?" Beauséjour said, laying the innuendo thick.

"Yes," Regan said. "Well until she threw me aside for Michael."

"She dated you before she dated Michael?"

"Immediately, you might say," Regan said, and the laid-back, casual humour had disappeared.

"Because?"

"I don't know, to be honest, but I suspect it had something to do with not being a prince," and this time there was pure contempt. "I know what you're thinking, on a lot of different levels, but the fact is I'm a grown-up adult, and a better person. Obviously, I was hurt and angry, but I'm not a child and know that people come and go. I accept that. And accordingly, I chose not to be a child and accepted the wedding invitation. I certainly didn't want to see her dead, no matter what had happened." He was sitting properly in the chair, his back erect and his eyes ablaze.

"You argued with the Princess at the wedding, correct?" Luna caught her breath slightly as the question came out. For a moment she wondered if Regan's new, aggressive approach would force a change in Beauséjour's behaviour, and now she realised she was right. There was the lawyer's metal again. Gone was the casual boho, replaced by the steely-eyes of a prosecutor about to catch a perp out. But Regan wasn't an idiot, and had detected the change as well. He was clearly comfortable being around lawyers. Consequently, he tempered his behaviour and paused before answering.

"Yes," he said, simply.

"Why?"

"I," Regan started, paused and then continued. "Was more hurt than I thought I'd be, I suppose." He sat back in his chair, a mood of defeat settling on him like a blanket of snow. "She has a strange way of getting inside your head. She can become very important to you very quickly. And then that's snapped away and you don't know how to react. You sort of want to set the fire going again. And then you realise there never was a fire. She's just very good at giving that illusion. I give her credit. She knows what she wants and she pursues it. When you find out that you're not it, however, it can be a little heartbreaking."

Luna was surprised at how sorry she felt for the man, but when she looked at Beauséjour the steel hadn't melted, and he wasn't going to give an inch.

"Did you write the note, Mr Regan?"

"I didn't have to, Mr Beauséjour," Regan replied. "I said what I had to face to face." It wasn't a retort, just a simple statement of fact. Beauséjour nodded.

"Thank you, Mr Regan."

Chapter Four

While the Interviews Took Place...

The Royal Arms, Reidon

I

There was a strange vibe permeating through each person; an odd feeling, a distinct sense of unease that came from sitting in a room knowing that someone in that room is a murderer. Knowing that someone is keeping something from everyone else, and potentially someone that you actually know quite well. Knowing that you yourself are keeping something from the rest of the room.

Knowing that you can't tell anyone that you committed a crime so heinous that there was a good chance you would never see the light of day again. Although, perhaps the murderer was more confident than that. Perhaps the murderer was actually sitting there thinking they had got away with it and no one would be able to stop them. After all, if you were confident enough to commit the crime, you were probably confident enough to believe you'd walk free.

Right?

Every single person sitting in the dining hall of The Royal Arms was in one of those positions, and they sat at their tables and chairs, making varied attempts to eat the food that had been prepared for them, though on edge, always risking glances around the room to see what the others were doing, how they were feeling, and what they might have to say for themselves. It was a catastrophe of cats; each one taking a bite from their dish, before looking warily around to see if someone was going to pounce.

Rifts were appearing in relationships long established, and assumed unassailable. Cracks in the veneer that had looked so perfect. The three royal siblings were keeping each other at a distance. Everyone could see it, even if they didn't know exactly what had taken place.

Cameron Regan wanted to know. He was interested to know what the royal siblings knew and what they suspected, but he was uncertain about approaching any of them, and which one he potentially could. Prince Michael was out of the question. They didn't have a good enough relationship at the best of times, and now was clearly not one of *those* times. Cameron Regan was also uncertain about approaching Prince Lucas. They barely knew each other, and truth to tell, Lucas irritated Regan quite a bit.

Which rather narrowed down his options.

"I wish we knew what that blasted man was doing," Clayton Reese said explosively, getting everyone's attention.

"Or what he wants with us," his wife added.

"And I wish one of you would own up to having written those letters," Reese continued. "They've got handwriting experts, you know. They'll identify you from the letters."

"One was typed," Lord Pero Petar said sardonically, and Regan had a little chuckle at Reese's bluster.

"I'm not talking about that one, for God's sake," and he shut up, finding himself on the backfoot.

"Are you happy with the meals?" Zakaria Barrera piped up, and everyone turned to him. "What? It is not an unreasonable question, surely?"

"It's the timing of your question that is awkward," Kendal Leigh said acidly.

"Oh, so I should wait until you have had a few days to forget about the meal and then ask you then? When I will no longer see any of you, but you are already spreading word of the food of Zakaria Barrera?"

"The food is perfect, Zakaria," Prince Michael said, ending the conversation. Barrera looked as though he wanted to engage more, but ultimately bit his tongue and sat back down.

When Inspector Danielle Kelinaw arrived and tapped the Reeses on the shoulders, dragging them into the little room that Beauséjour had turned into his office, there was a ripple of unease that ran through the remaining guests. Burton jumped up to follow, but ended up resting against the wall, possibly with the intention of hearing what was going on. He was probably in the best position to do so, but that didn't necessarily stop the gossip.

At the main table, Dione Lora turned to Kendal Leigh and whispered to her.

"Do you think Burton is the killer?"

"Why?" Kendal asked, curiously.

"Well, he's hanging around that door," Dione pointed out.

"He probably thinks they are doing his job," Kendal said a little dismissively.

"But he would be the prefect killer, don't you think?" Dione continued, trying to press home the point. Kendal looked at her with a frown.

"Well, maybe. I mean, the perfect killer would be the Prince, surely?" Kendal replied.

"Oh, don't be ridiculous, Kendal," Dione snorted, her voice raising, causing the three men at the table to glance at them.

"Well, I mean, he was the person that discovered the body."

"Except I was there as well," Dione said, pointedly.

"I didn't say I was ruling you out, did I?" Kendal said sweetly, and the blood ran from Dione's face.

"You don't think that I did it, do you?" she asked, panicked.

"Suspect everyone," Kendal smirked, and Dione bit her lip.

II

Princess Stephanie hovered near the door to the side corridor, as though she wanted to go through, but wasn't sure whether she should. The situation was starting to get grim, with the Reeses returning, and the Inspector now taking the Vladans away. Stephanie narrowed her eyes at this, but did nothing more, given that she was so far away from what was being said.

However, she was clearly agitated. She chewed on her bottom lip, her mind clearly turning over at a hundred miles per hour, trying to make a decision on something. She was so deep in her thinking that she didn't even notice Cameron Regan had come up to her, until he spoke.

"Penny for them?" he said.

"Sorry?" she looked at him blankly.

"Oh, no, I'm sorry. You might not have the same sayings over here. We offer pennies for people's thoughts. At least that's the saying. It just means would you like to talk about it." Cameron Regan said nothing more, and indeed gave a slight smile.

"Oh, no," Stephanie said. "I am just unsettled. This is all quite…" She paused, trying to find the right English word.

"Unnerving?" Regan offered, and she nodded.

"Yes, that. Are you not unnerved?"

"Perhaps a little," Regan agreed. "Unfortunately, my past with Lauren makes me a prime target, I suspect. And that Beauséjour chap seems the dog with a bone sort. He's not going to let it go until everything is explained. You can tell the type. I bet he has his CD collection all ordered alphabetically."

"CD collection?" Stephanie asked.

"God, now you make me feel old," Regan chuckled. "How much younger than your brother are you?"

"Oh, about ten years," Stephanie smiled. "My parents were keen to have big spaces between our births. My mother, the former Queen, had Michael when she was relatively young. Me at a more sensible age, and Lucas…well, he was probably not planned, I suspect." Stephanie smiled, and Regan smiled back.

"I rather like your smile," he said. "You've spent a lot of the day looking annoyed, but it's nice to know that there's a chirpier side to you."

"You're very charming, Mr Regan," the Princess said, touching his arm slightly. "But I'm not stupid. I don't know whether you are trying to flirt with me because you are interested, or if you are trying to get information out of me. Or perhaps in the hope that I will side with you."

"It wasn't really any of those," Regan admitted, "but I take your point. You don't trust me."

"Not even remotely," the Princess replied. "I must keep my wits about me," she continued. "Because I am not going to fall into anyone's traps. Not Professor Beauséjour's, and not yours." She touched him on the arm again, clearly and deliberately, but then turned and walked away from him.

Cameron Regan watched her go, his mind turning over.

III

Just before Cameron Regan had been summoned, Inspector Kelinaw had a word with a number of the staff, and soon, the waiters began taking plates and remains away, whilst also indicating that they needed to rearrange the room.

The staff had already been interviewed by Kelinaw thoroughly as earlier Beauséjour had suggested she get a rough timeline of their movements and whether or not anyone had disappeared for any length of time. In truth, he had said to her, he doubted that any of them were genuine suspects, but it paid to be careful, and so Kelinaw had done her duty and gone through the staff, starting with Tehmia Masri and then working her way through the kitchen staff and waiters. Beauséjour had been right; everyone had each other under surveillance and there was no real opportunity for a single person to slip away unnoticed. Each person had been with someone else that was working with them to get the jobs done as quickly and efficiently as possible.

Once again, though, the guests were concerned, but by now they weren't afraid of letting people know what they were thinking. As the staff moved forward and invited people to stand so the tables could be moved, very few people held back on their opinions. As usual, Beddows and Amy Birman remained to one side, dutifully waiting over their master as was required.

"It's all getting just a little bit silly now, don't you think, old chap?" Count Vladan said, as the waiter explained that they needed to move the tables.

"You should have a drink," Dr Kilman advised. "I'm finding that this whole day is going a lot easier with a drink, I can assure you."

"Just the one?" Lord Pero asked with a smirk. Kilman turned to him, somewhat surprised to find the man standing beside him.

"When did you get here?"

"When I was asked to move so they could move the bridal table. I have no idea why everything is being rearranged, though I'm sure it's got something to do with that annoying professor."

"I'm sure you're right," Count Vladan sighed. Lord Pero offered his arm, and the older man gratefully took it, leaning on him. "Honestly, it's definitely not me," he complained a little. "I couldn't stab her if I wanted to."

"Of course it's not you," his wife snapped archly. "As if anyone with any nobility would be involved in something so tawdry. It's one of these others, or a staff member, no doubt."

"I hope you're not including me in that," Kilman said, before taking another swig of his drink.

"I'm sure you weren't in a room alone with Lauren," Lord Pero said, and this time the smirk was very clear on his face. "You wouldn't be allowed to be, would you?"

"What the hell is that supposed to mean?" Kilman spluttered.

"Oh, I must have misheard," the taller man said, lashings of smarm very obvious.

By now the guests were being forced together, as the staff moved chairs around, and the tables were manhandled. The awkwardness was obvious, and none of them were interested in hiding it anymore. It had reached that part of evening where everyone wanted to go home and get away from the situation they had found themselves in.

"We're veritable prisoners here," Clayton Reese muttered under his breath, though it was loud enough for everyone to have heard.

"We must be patient," Prince Michael said calmly.

"We *are* being patient," Countess Vladan snipped drily.

"By accusing the staff of being the killers?" Zakaria Barrera said, and Countess Vladan turned to him imperiously.

"You watch your tongue," she snapped.

"Oh, because you are concerned now, yes?" Barrera said, and there was a note of triumph in his voice. "You know what I saw, yes. You are unhappy, I think, you have been all night, after you leave the Princess."

"I don't know what you're talking about," Countess Vladan said dismissively. "You're just talking about silly things. Unimportant. I can barely understand you."

"Please," Prince Michael said. "Please. Until this is sorted, we are not going anywhere. If we descend into a fight, then it's going to make this a very long process." He started to trail off for a moment, and then seemed to pull himself together and looked at the group. Reluctantly they mostly nodded, accepting what he said.

"I just want to be able to sit down again," muttered Blake Reese.

"Hopefully Beauséjour will be back soon," her husband said softly.

IV

The Prince had been distracted by the somewhat bizarre sight of Solomon Burton wiggling a finger at him, trying to get his attention, presumably. Puzzled, Prince Michael stepped away from the group and casually went towards the antechamber where Burton was trying to eavesdrop on the conversation inside. To his surprise, Burton moved towards the corner of the room, and, a little annoyed, Michael followed him.

"What do you want, Burton?"

"Your Highness, I just wanted to say," Burton said, and then lowered his voice dramatically. "I just wanted to say I have your back, and I just wanted you to know that."

"What?" the Prince replied, puzzled.

"I overheard you saying that you and the Princess would have a chance to be together soon, and I promise I'll tell Beauséjour as soon as I can. Then maybe he can release you and you can go home."

Prince Michael looked at him blankly, clearly not understanding at all what Burton had been talking about, and for a moment, the bulky, bald man was unsure of himself, as if he had perhaps said something he shouldn't have. However, before he could do anything about it, the Prince suddenly smiled.

"Oh, yes," he said. "My goodness in all the confusion I had completely forgotten saying that to Lauren. Oh, how wrong I was. But yes, yes, of course, of course." He nodded, a thankful smile on his face. "Have you told Professor Beauséjour that you heard that? You haven't, yet?" The Prince raised an eyebrow, and again Burton suddenly got the feeling he wasn't entirely in on the conversation.

"No, not yet," Burton said.

"Don't worry about it, Solomon. Honestly, I have every confidence in Professor Beauséjour. I know that he's a good chap, so he'll be fine. But thank you so much for your loyalty. You've always been there for me, and I appreciate it a great deal. It's probably high time we rewarded you for that loyalty, don't you think? And now that I'm king, we can sort that out."

"Now you're king?" Burton said, hesitantly.

"Well, when I'm crowned, obviously. And I can be, now that I'm married."

"Oh yes, of course," Burton nodded. "So, keep it to myself?"

"Well, unless someone tries to lie about me, then by all means, bring it up. But otherwise, I trust Beauséjour. Almost as much as a I trust you," he added with a genial grin. He shook Burton's hand. "We should get back to the group," the Prince said. "Unless there's more you needed to…" He indicated the antechamber, and Burton shook his head.

"No, no, not at all. I was just. I wasn't…"

"I understand. Loyal to the end, Solomon," the Prince smiled, and turned to head back to the group, leaving behind a very happy Burton. Give the Prince his due, Burton reflected, he was a good employer.

V

"You seem unhappy," Kendal Leigh said.

She had followed the mystery woman to the window where, now she thought about it, the woman had spent a lot of her free time. The window was shuttered, so there didn't seem to be an awful lot to see, but it didn't stop her.

"I'm Kendal. I'm not sure we've met."

"Lady Jacinta Daniels," came the reply, and there was a slight smile that went with it.

"Oh, you're with Prince Michael's side," Kendal suddenly said, understanding why she was so mysterious.

"Yes, just a ring in to make up the numbers, really," Lady Jacinta said. "Though I did know of Lauren. She seemed nice."

"Yes, very nice. She was one of my best friends. Not that I have a lot, but yeah," Kendal nodded.

"It must be a horrible time for you," Lady Jacinta said.

"Oh, yes," Kendal agreed. "I can't quite believe it, if I'm honest. I think I keep forgetting about it. That's weird, isn't it? I just sort of forget that she hasn't been murdered and then someone says something and I remember and I get that shock again."

"I understand completely how you feel," Lady Jacinta said. "Like, you think, oh I should go and tell Lauren that this crazy shit is going on, and then you think, oh I can't. Because she's what the crazy shit is all about."

"She'd have loved this. The drama," grinned Kendal.

"Like a duck to water," Lady Jacinta agreed, and the pair laughed, before both stopping and looking around guiltily.

"I'm glad I came over to talk to you," Kendal said.

"Me too," Lady Jacinta replied, and she grabbed the other woman's hand and held it tight.

They were still holding on when Professor Beauséjour re-entered the room.

Chapter Five

The Seance

The Royal Arms, Reidon

Luna Rochique fought to suppress a smile when she saw that staff had moved the tables in the dining room towards the outer edges of the room in order to free up a central space. All the chairs had been arranged into a circle. The only person who seemed completely at ease with the new layout was, of course, Axton Beauséjour, who had requested it. Every other person seemed to fall between outrage and astonishment.

Beauséjour was already seated at one of the chairs, and Luna moved to sit beside him. She wasn't sure what was going to happen, but she was absolutely certain that she didn't want to be seated anywhere other than beside Beauséjour. If there was going to be anything of bizarre happening, she was certain it would be near him.

As if they didn't have a choice (and in truth, they largely didn't), the other guests also sat down around the room. Madame Jindra was beside Beauséjour, and on her left was the Prince, with Pero, Shelby, Dione and Kendal seated to his left. Regan had sat beside Luna, with the Reeses beside him, and Lady Jacinta beside them. The Vladans were also together beside Kendal, and the younger Prince and Princess were beside them. Dr Kilman was beside the Princess, and beside him was Borna Vanya. For the first time, Luna noticed that she and Kilman seemed to be muttering to each other. Between Vanya and the Reeses sat Burton and Barrera.

"Perhaps," Beauséjour suddenly said, "we should make a little room and invite Mr Beddows and Ms Birman to join us. You should as well, Inspector." Beauséjour looked across the room to where the staff were waiting patiently, having rearranged the furniture, and at his nod, they came forward with three seats. Their annoyance levels increasing, everyone began to move their seats back, so that the circle could now include the new guests.

Not that they seemed to particularly appreciate being asked to join in, Luna noted. Well, not Beddows, at least, who was clearly muttering under his breath.

"Entirely inappropriate," were the only two words he uttered clearly as he sat himself down.

The room was obviously the way Beauséjour wanted, and with the complete change of space, came with it a change of attitude. The seating of the last three members had a strange effect on the assembled guests, with each and every one of them seemingly losing their frustration with what was going on, and replacing it with an abject silence. No one was quite sure why they shouldn't be speaking, but they just knew that they shouldn't. Not a single word was uttered, and Luna watched when Clayton Reese turned to his wife, and she held up a single finger to her lips. The lights appeared to dim, and Luna wondered if it had actually happened, of if she was feeling the drama of what was about to happen. She realised she hadn't checked the time for a while, and guessed that it must definitely be dark outside. Beauséjour had created a very specific atmosphere, and the consequence was that everyone was a little on edge, and just a little bit nervous.

"Madame Pét'a," Beauséjour said – and his voice rang out despite the fact it wasn't loud – "is going to indulge us all with a séance." He turned to look to the woman, who smiled, almost apologetically, and made one final attempt to correct her hat, before standing up, bringing herself to the top of her height.

"I have the ability to contact the dead," she announced dramatically, and Luna fought to roll her eyes as she realised that there was a glass of wine in her hand. "I'm going to contact Princess Lauren herself." There was an unsurprising rumbling around the room, and Luna clearly caught a number of people speaking.

"This is an outrage!" was all Clayton Reese could supply, while the Prince was more vocal.

"I can't believe that anyone would have the audacity," he said, and the emotion on his face was raw.

"Please, please," Beauséjour held up his hands to stop the discussion. He turned to Prince Michael. "I'm asking you to trust me. Give me this latitude. Let's see if Madame Pét'a is remotely true to her word." Michael looked at him, and

Beauséjour raised an eyebrow ever so slightly, to which the prince nodded slowly. Jindra also nodded, gratefully, before comically double taking as she seemed to realise that Beauséjour's words held as much doubt in her abilities as the less subtle members of the group.

"I am already in touch with her. I have already summoned her," she said with a tone of self-importance, though it was quickly shot down.

"And?" Lord Pero demanded, imperiously.

"She says there is much love in this room."

"Of course there is," Blake Reese said, and there was a murmur of agreement, as different people looked at each other, as if to dare they challenge the sentiment.

"But there is evil here," Madame Jindra added, and the murmur was quelled, quickly. "Much evil lying in people's hearts." She paused, gazing around the room, then closed her eyes and put her free hand to forehead, arranging her fingers in a curious pattern. "Princess Lauren recognises some of her previous loves," she intoned.

"Surely none of her previous loves are here?" Beauséjour smirked slightly, much to Luna's annoyance.

"I'm sure I don't count in that group," Luna muttered.

"The Prince," Madame Jindra declared.

"He was going to marry her," Borna Vanya said. Everyone looked at her, somewhat surprised to hear her speak out. "Of course he loves her," she added, slightly quieter, her face a little red.

"I don't think she means that Prince, does she Prince Lucas?" Beauséjour said, fixing his gaze on the younger royal. For the first time, Luna realised that Lucas had fallen into Beauséjour's sights.

"I..I mean…" Prince Lucas stumbled, unsure of what else to say.

"Prince Lucas was in love with the Princess and begged her not to marry Prince Michael," Madame Jindra said, her eyes still closed, her arm still stretched out like a scarecrow. Prince Michael, however, was not so composed.

"I knew it!" the groom barked, and Luna suddenly realised that while he may have suspected his brother was in love with his bride, he hadn't guessed just how far that love had gone.

"I'm sorry, but I adored her!" Lucas said, and Michael looked as though he were about to rise, but Lord Pero put a hand on his arm, bringing him back to the chair. The tension between the brothers was palpable, and Luna guessed that Madame Jindra had got it very right. Was it a lucky guess, she wondered, or had she overheard something, or seen something that pointed her in the right direction.

She couldn't, after all, actually be communicating with Princess Lauren.

Could she?

Succubus to steal your heart…

"And she wasn't the only member of the Royal Family to love the Princess," Madame Jindra continued, but before she could provide another expose, she was beaten to the punch.

"I had an *encounter* with her," Princess Stephanie announced, and there was a slight gasp around the room, though Stephanie rolled her eyes at the supposed shock. "It was hardly love," she added, raising an eyebrow at her brothers. "But it does go to show what sort of person she is."

"And what sort of person is that, Princess?" Beauséjour asked softly. This time when the silence fell, there was an anticipation to it as the ramifications of what Beauséjour was asking sunk in for everyone. Even Princess Stephanie looked as though she thought perhaps the situation had gone too far, but then she seemed to make a decision. A commitment.

"She wasn't in love with anyone. This woman is a fraud." Stephanie cast a savage glance at Madame Jindra who finally opened her eyes to catch it. "If she could see into Lauren's heart she would know there was no love there. We all know it. Why are we pretending?" Stephanie crossed her arms and sat back in her chair, unrepentant with what she had just said.

"She's right," said Regan, out of nowhere. Stephanie gave him a look of appreciation for his support, though it was clearly not echoed by everyone as a new voice spoke out.

"You shut your mouth," snapped Hunter Shelby.

"Oh please. I loved her once. I gave her my everything. But once she had taken all she wanted from me, she moved on to a bigger fish. And then to rub it in she invited me to the wedding. I'm under no illusions as to who Lauren

Foster truly was." Suddenly there was an intake of breath, and Amy Birman sat up straight.

"I saw you fight with her! Before we left for the reception!" she said, breathless.

"Yes. I confronted her. I told her what I thought of her I made it clear exactly what a nasty piece of work she was." Like Stephanie he had committed, clearly with no regrets as to what he had just said.

"And the letter signed CR!" Kendal Leigh realised.

"I didn't send that," Regan said. "But no, I didn't like her. She was awful."

"She was anything but!" Hunter Shelby suddenly blurted out. "She was incredible."

"Though you are biased, Mr Shelby. After all, you loved her as well, correct?" Axton Beauséjour looked at him from across the room.

"What?" Hunter paused, shocked. "I…" he started, but couldn't finish. Luna realised she hadn't been looking at Shelby when Prince Lucas had announced his love, but she made sure to take in the younger prince's reaction this time, and sure enough, Prince Lucas was slack-jawed, a mixture of jealousy, anger and hurt across his face.

And he wasn't even the prince marrying Lauren. God only knew what Prince Michael must have been feeling.

"You are on the list of loves!" Madame Jindra suddenly intoned and her hand swung around to point at Hunter.

"No, I mean, I…" Hunter stuttered, but was interrupted by an unexpected voice.

"Oh, come on Hunter," Lord Pero said wearily. "We all knew it."

"That's not," Hunter started again, but again Lord Pero interrupted him. However, this time it was different. It was though a floodgate had opened and Lord Pero Petar, weary of all those around him and all that was going on, had had enough and decided to simply lay his cards on the table.

"The amount of people snapping at her heels," he said, and the disgust in his voice was obvious. "That you did as well was pathetic." Hunter looked as though he had been slapped in the face and didn't know how to respond. Both princes as well looked stung, clearly not expecting this from the best man.

"Anyone else want to add themselves to the list of lovers? Or perhaps Madame Pét'a has more names." Beauséjour said, after leaving the silence hang in the room for a moment.

"There are those that sort to harm her," Madame Jindra said, waving her hand regally. Once again, her eyes closed and she seemed to be about to point at someone in the room specifically.

"Oh please," Princess Stephanie said. "There are those that sought to expose her." Luna flashed a look at the Princess, and then at Beauséjour, who remained quiet. Luna wondered if had been expecting this reaction, if maybe the idea of bottling up everyone, and in consequence forcing them to bottle up their feelings and opinions, had been a goal from the beginning. Like an irritating sore that continued to itch and itch, had Beauséjour simply decided to see how long it would take before people started to scratch?

"The Count and Countess…" Madame Jindra said dramatically, but Princess Stephanie wasn't to be swayed.

"I told them the truth about Lauren," Stephanie said, and Luna noticed Beauséjour frown a little.

"We were going to help Princess Stephanie reveal the truth," the Countess announced.

"What truth, exactly?" Beauséjour said.

"She just wanted Michael for his money," Stephanie said, and it seemed to be a relief to release something that had been bottled up for so long. "She slept with Cameron to get his money, but then found our family. She tried to seduce Lucas, she got me into bed, but it was Michael who had what she really wanted. I told the Count and Countess and we agreed to do something about it. We were going to expose her!"

"And so I spoke to her about it," the Countess said, and like a series of dominoes, the first had fallen and was now knocking down the others after it.

"Hang on," Prince Lucas said. "I overheard you. It wasn't that. I overheard you saying something about a million a year!"

"I told you someone would hear you," the Count said, turning to his wife.

"No, but," the woman said, but couldn't find the words to continue.

And another domino fell.

"Emília!" Princess Stephanie said, horrified.

"I," the Countess started, but clearly was overtaken by events. "I don't know what to say," she whined.

"Then say nothing, Emília," snarled her husband. "For once in your life, shut your mouth!" Luna risked a glance at Beauséjour, and wasn't surprised to see he had a small smile on his face.

"I wouldn't feel too badly. You're not the only crooks at the table, I suspect," he said, unable to contain the grin that his smile grew into. "Would you agree Madame Pét'a?"

"Mr and Mrs Reese also confronted the Princess," came the reply.

"Now, hold on. We were here to give the girl away!" Clayton Reese growled.

"No!" boomed Madame Jindra. "You had tried to ruin Princess Lauren's parents' company. You stole her inheritance. She was blackmailing you!"

"Oh, arrant rubbish," Reese growled. "If that were the case, why come here?"

"Perhaps, now that the Princess had a new benefactor and didn't need your money to survive, she had nothing more to protect the world from. Perhaps she was going to expose you," Beauséjour challenged him.

This time Clayton Reese leapt up, and his fists were balled. He launched himself at Beauséjour, who stepped back, raising his cane to defend himself, but to everyone's surprise, Reese was suddenly on the floor, Solomon Burton's knee in his back.

"Get off me," snarled Reese.

"You get a grip," Burton returned, and everyone watched as Reese's tension almost immediately went limp. Burton got up, and Reese pulled himself up with a degree of difficulty. He didn't take his eyes off Beauséjour, glaring at him like a child told he couldn't have a toy.

"Clayton made a mistake," Blake Reese said, and everyone's eyes turned to her. "He got greedy. We got greedy. I won't let him take the fall alone. We thought we could have everything once Lauren's father passed. It's too late for cover ups now. But Lauren found out, and we were paying for our mistake dearly."

"And you're right," Reese said, slumping down in his chair. "She had decided that she didn't need us, so she was going to turn us over to the police. Well done, *Professor*."

"The note! The CR!" Kendal exclaimed, and Luna was suddenly caught up in the moment.

"Perhaps the B on the mirror stood for Blake?" Luna added.

"We had every reason to kill her," Clayton said. "And yes, I sent the note, and I was secretly happy she had been murdered. But we didn't kill her. And I can promise you, Blake would never have been involved. She was always telling me we were doing the wrong thing." He looked at Blake with what seemed to be an apology, but she simply smiled and reached across to take his hand.

"It seems that the everyone either loved the Princess, or despised her," Beauséjour said, the smile again playing around his lips.

"I didn't *love* her in that sense. She was just my best friend," Dione pointed out.

"Same for me," agreed the other bridesmaid, but this was ignored by Madame Jindra who was now in full flight, and like some sort of velvet hurricane, she swung around, her gown spinning and almost hitting Beauséjour, she pointed at Dione, impressively managing to keep her eyes shut all the time.

"No!" she bellowed. "You told the Princess he didn't deserve Prince Michael!"

"What? How do you…" Dione's mouth dropped open. However, before she could continue to speak, Solomon Burton suddenly looked up, his eyes lighting up.

"I heard the Prince say that they would get a chance to be together soon," he said, the cogs in his brain turning slowly. "I thought he was talking to Princess Lauren, but now I think about it…"

"Princess Lauren never left her room, and the Prince never walked down the corridor?" Beauséjour suggested, and Burton nodded. Luna shot a glance at the Prince, who seemed remarkably composed. Almost amused, she reflected.

"That's not true!" Dione said.

"So, you've never had romantic feelings for the Prince?" Beauséjour asked her.

"Of course not," Dione said, but there wasn't anyone in the room who didn't notice the lack of conviction in her voice.

"Dione." Kendall only spoke a single word, but it was enough to cause Dione's eyes to well up.

"Why…?"

"Because the truth is coming out, isn't it," Kendall said softly. "This psychic has all our secrets. Lying now isn't going to help." Dione looked left and right, but the tears began to flow freely and she buried her face in her hands. The Prince said nothing, keeping his composure, his jaw set, his face dispassionate.

"And there is another to expose!" Madame Jindra continued, not remotely losing momentum. "Dr Kilman!" Unlike the Prince, however, Kilman most certainly did not remain composed. Luna remembered Beauséjour making a comment earlier about the man's drinking, and she wondered if that contributed to his anger.

"What? I didn't kill her!" he shouted.

"You wanted her dead!" Madame Jindra said, and her eyes opened for the first time, boring into Kilman's skull.

"She was horrid." Kilman said, waving a hand. "To everyone. Just ask Beddows. Or Burton."

"I have nothing to say," Beddows said, before adding, "and neither does Birman."

"What about you, Mr Burton?" The burly security guard looked across the room at the Prince, and then looked at the floor, before speaking.

"Well, she was pretty horrible. I mean, Beddows, may wish to be stiff upper lipped and all, but Kilman's not wrong. She treated the staff like rubbish." Beauséjour nodded as thought it was exactly the answer he expected.

"Horrible enough to kill?" he pondered.

"She made our lives a misery!" Kilman said, his face red.

"Mr Beddows?" Beauséjour prompted.

"I…" Beddows looked uncertain, which impressed Beauséjour. He was the definitive gentleman's gentleman. He couldn't lie, but he also couldn't speak ill of the Master. Or Mistress. He was, however, saved by the bell.

"Relax Beddows," Lord Pero suddenly said, and the Prince looked at him, the hint of betrayal on his face. "She was the worst. Horrible enough to kill? Well, I for one would have done anything to get her out of our lives. Out of Michael's life. She treated him terribly. No wonder he had an affair. It was the only way someone would show him some love. I wouldn't feel bad if Burton or Beddows killed her. I could never understand why Hunter loved her. She was the worst." Luna noted the confirmation of the affair, intrigued that Lord Pero knew of it. Presumably Dione, she reflected. Interesting, as Beauséjour might say.

"But she had reason to hate Kilman in particular!" Madame Jindra continued, which brought Kilman back to full scarlet.

"Excuse me?"

"You only examined her once. And there was a reason for that!" Her eyes were open, and again they bore into the doctor with a laser focus.

"This is slander! How dare you!" At this point Kilman, got up, but there was suddenly a cane in his chest and he looked down to see that Beauséjour had also risen, bring up his cane to stop the man going further.

"Calm down, Dr Kilman," Beauséjour said. "It seems we are at an interesting point. It seems nearly everyone wanted her dead, because of the way she treated them; either throwing them away from love, because she thought they were beneath her, or because she was using them to feather her own nest. And some deserved the treatment they received." He paused looking at each member of the reception in turn. Some, like Lord Pero and Kilman met his glance, but many lowered their eyes, unable to take in what was being said. "It's now just down to expose the last few, I think," Beauséjour said, and he turned to Madame Jindra with a smile.

"There is no more on the Princess' list," she said, puzzled.

"It's interesting you keep saying list, Madame Pét'a," Beauséjour said. "Because that's exactly what you're working from, isn't it?"

Suddenly everyone in the room was no longer concentrating on themselves. Beauséjour had provided a target, and each guest, desperate to no longer be in Beauséjour's gaze, zoomed in, curious to know where he was going.

"What?" the medium stuttered, but Luna could see the fear in her eyes.

"You're a complete fraud," Beauséjour announced. "You aren't contacting anyone. You just happened to have several lists, with all the shocking information on it. Memorised it in your little noggin and then pretended you were in touch with the dead." He tapped the side of his head.

"That's…you can't back that up." Madame Jindra said, with as much confidence as she could muster. But there was still hesitation in her voice.

"Except I have the lists," Beauséjour smiled. "I stole them from your purse earlier this evening." Luna watched him reach into his pocket and pull out some folded pieces of paper. Madame Jindra's eyes widened. Luna suddenly recalled Beauséjour picking up Jindra's bag earlier when she had dropped it. He had put things into the bag and had seen the Tarot cards, but he must have also taken the lists at the same time. Not for the first time, Luna found herself somewhat admiring the man's gall.

"You…" Jindra started, but it went nowhere.

"But who gave her the lists?" For the first time Prince Michael spoke up, and Beauséjour turned and crossed over to him.

"Oh, well," he shrugged. "Someone close to the Princess. Someone who walked away largely unscathed from tonight's little show." He walked slowly around the circle stopping in front of Dione.

"Well, I didn't walk away unscathed," she said, her voice clearly still recovering from her earlier humiliation.

"You did not," agreed Beauséjour. "You also didn't encourage the truth to come out." She glared at him, but Beauséjour wasn't looking. Instead, he turned to the person beside her. "Isn't that right, Ms Leigh?"

"What? I didn't mean," Kendal started, but Beauséjour simply held up a hand, and rather grandly produced some folded-up pieces of paper from his pocket.

"The lists are emails. Your name is on the top. You don't have to be a genius to work that out." The silence in the room was deafening. Luna found she couldn't help but feel the butterflies in her stomach, almost scared of what would happen next. "Are you actually cousins?" Beauséjour asked, a smile on his face.

"She needed…" Kendal began, but again Beauséjour cut her off.

"Jindra? Jindra Pét'a? She needed something?" Beauséjour's eyes narrowed. "I'm sure she did. After all, she was being blackmailed by the Princess as well, weren't you?" He turned to the medium and this time there was real, raw emotion on the woman's face.

"I'm glad she's dead!" No more performance, just the real person, exposed in front of everyone to see. Almost as if she knew, Madame Jindra pulled her hat off, tired of the stupid unattached fruit.

"That's what Lauren was like," Kendal insisted. "She used people. She just found something and would use it. And it's not like Jindra even had money. Lauren was literally playing with her for her own amusement."

But Beauséjour had seemed to lose interest in her. Instead, he had turned to someone else in the circle, and when Luna looked to where he was going, her memory sparked.

"The real question, of course, is Lady Jacinta," Beauséjour said. "Who has remained silent this entire time."

"I'm sure I saw her talk to the Princess," Luna muttered, though loud enough for Beauséjour to hear. "I definitely did." Yes, when she was with Dana Spectra, they had looked out the window… "She made the Princess cry. Just before we left for the reception hall!"

"Who are you, Lady Jacinta?" Beauséjour asked.

"I told you I'm a cousin," the woman replied.

"Who's just here for the party. What did you think of Princess Lauren?"

"We never really met," Lady Jacinta said dismissively.

"But you made her cry," Beauséjour replied, and Luna felt a slight note of delight that he believed her.

"I honestly don't know why that happened," Lady Jacinta admitted.

"And you didn't want her dead?"

"Why should I?" Beauséjour looked at her, as though seriously taking her answer into consideration. He suddenly stopped and looked around the room, again taking in each and every person. Luna could almost hear his brain analysing the data, sorting it and rearranging it so it made the correct pattern. He lost focus on the room, his eyes twitching, as though he were seeing the information falling into place.

"Oh," Luna said softly, and she saw it. His grand version of sudoku, with every person a number that needed to fall into different patterns. Different patterns where everyone had to slot in precisely. That's what he was doing!

"Why should you?" he repeated, loud enough for everyone to hear. Then suddenly he stopped. "I think I know who the killer is," he grinned.

Interlude

Lucas Regrets The Future

The Royal Arms, Reidon

Four hours ago

Prince Lucas made his way down the hallway, feeling a little bit nervous, which was strange because he was a Prince of the Realm and he really shouldn't be nervous about anything. Nonetheless he needed to talk to Lauren because, well because they had things that needed to be sorted out. When he approached the door to the corridor, he had to pause because that idiot Burton didn't seem to be anywhere around. For a moment, Lucas felt a surge of power flood through him, and he wanted to reprimand the man for his incompetence, but as he pushed the door open and walked through, he dismissed it. He had more important things to worry about than the castle staff. That was Michael's responsibility, ultimately.

Coincidentally, he paused when he heard Michael's voice.

"We'll have a chance to be together soon," Michael was saying, and Lucas paused, wondering where the sound was coming from. There were a few rooms in the corridor, and he knew Lauren's was at the end, which was presumably where Michael was as well. There were a lot of people around, popping in to see the new Princess (he was fairly certain he had seen those Americans godparents of hers entering the corridor as he approached), which probably explained what Michael was talking about.

Lucas wondered if he should bother going to see Lauren, given Micheal was there, but then he decided that his brother might go, giving him a chance to be alone with the new Princess.

Resolve filling him, he walked down the corridor, and was a little surprised to hear the Reeses' voices rather than his brother's, coming from the Princess' room.

"I cannot believe you're acting like this, Lauren," he heard Clayton Reese say, very clearly, but there was a murmur, and then suddenly Reese burst out of the room, ostensibly in a fit of pique. Lucas raised an eyebrow as the man stormed past him, and then Blake Reese followed, smiling apologetically at him.

Very odd, he mused.

He waited a few moments, but Michael didn't seem to be leaving, and so, with nerves building up inside him, he entered the Princess' room.

"Lauren?" he said, as he entered, and was astonished to see Michael wasn't there at all. For a moment, Lucas was disorientated, and he looked around, almost as if he expected Michael to creep up behind him and shout "surprise!" Lauren herself was seated behind her table, and he couldn't really see her for the mirror. He wanted to move forward, but he felt strangely uncomfortable doing so without being asked. "Lauren?" he repeated, but she gave no answer.

Was she annoyed at him?

"Look," he started, and then realized that she probably was. Of course she was. He was going to bring up something he shouldn't on her wedding day of all things. "Look I know you don't want me to mention *us*," he said, and looked around, wondering if Michael might just walk in.

Where had his voice come from earlier?

Was it even his voice he had heard?

"The thing is," he went on, "I just can't let us go. I mean I know I have to and I know I should, especially now that you're married, but I just…" There was still no response. Lucas lowered his head, and realized she must have been very, very angry with him. "Please don't ignore me, Lauren," he said, but it sounded pathetic, even to his ears.

He wondered if he should say anymore, but he could just tell she was not going to talk to him any further. The coldness from the woman was tangible.

"I'm…I'm sorry," he finally said. Still no response. Tears stung at his eyes, but he turned and started to walk out.

What a way to end it, he sighed, sadly.

PART FOUR

SO HELP ME GOD

Chapter One

Playing The Cards That Are Dealt

The Royal Arms, Reidon

If the tension in the room earlier had been mild, it was now very tangible. You could almost taste the distrust in the air, thought Luna, as though Zakaria Barrera had created a new dish out of the raw emotions that were on display; the distinct aroma of suspicion and fear wafting around the room, as potent as any herb or spice that had been put on the meals. But the thing was, Luna mused, you couldn't really tell who was feeling what. Was that suspicion on the face of Princess Stephanie, or was it fear?

"Before we begin, I have three questions," Axton Beauséjour said. He didn't have to speak very loudly, because at the end of the day everyone was paying very close attention to what he was saying. "Ms Lora, did you see a glass in the room when you found the Princess?" It wasn't the first time he had latched onto this particular detail, and Luna wondered why he was obsessing over it.

"No," the chief bridesmaid shook her head. "I don't think so. I mean, I wasn't looking for one." She paused to think before continuing. "No, actually, no because I looked around and I would've seen one." Beauséjour nodded, as though it were the answer he had expected. He paced around the room, before stopping at Clayton Reese, who looked at him with his steely grey eyes.

"Mr Reese, what did the Princess say to you when you had your argument? Exactly if you please." Reese looked as though he were about to explode, but then brought himself back into check.

"I just," he started, before shrugging. "I don't know. I think I said you can't hold us to ransom or something like that and she said…well, I think she just said no, or…I don't know…"

"You're sure she said no?" Beauséjour pressed.

"I'm…no, actually she said nothing," Reese suddenly said. "She said nothing. She was rude and ignorant and said nothing. Not for the first time, so, typical Lauren." Beauséjour again nodded, and again it was as though it were the answer he had expected. Finally, he paused in front of Amy Birman, who looked up at him, her eyes wide with worry.

"Ms Birman, why did the Princess want to change into a red dress?"

"Oh?" Amy looked startled, but then collected herself. "The Princess didn't want to wear her bridal dress to the reception. She wanted to make an impression with something more powerful." Beauséjour didn't react to this at all, but after a moment he moved to the centre of the room. Luna had to admit that she was on tenterhooks. For a moment it seemed so surreal, like a classic mystery was about to solved, and she wondered if Beauséjour had staged it this way on purpose. However, the truth was someone had died. And perhaps the most insightful person in the room was about to reveal precisely who the killer was.

No wonder everyone had suddenly decided to behave themselves.

"From the outset this case has been one of lies," Beauséjour started. "Everyone associated with the Princess was lying about something; every one of them giving us a piece of information that was not true, and it wasn't until others were pressed that those lies were finally exposed." He stopped, looking around at the group, accusing them all. "But more than that, there was the issue of the clues. There were far too many clues. It was more lies, more obfuscation. Rather than hiding the clues by trying to get rid of them, the murderer decided to hide the clues by surrounding them by more clues, hoping that we wouldn't see the trees for the forest." Again, he stopped, and this time Luna knew he was being deliberately dramatic.

"And they almost succeeded," he said softly. "Let's go back to just before the Princess left for the reception. Before Ms Lora and Ms Kendal got in the car that would bring them, they saw me talking to the Princess. Offering my congratulations. But then, more people spoke to the Princess. Two more, in fact. Ms Birman saw Mr Regan talk with the Princess, though Mr Regan's conversation was a little more heated than the one I had. And then Ms Birman got in the car, but the Princess had one more person to speak to. Lady Jacinta, as seen by Ms Rochique, met with the Princess and seemed to make her cry." He paused, and then turned to look directly at Luna. "Except, when she got in the car, she wasn't upset at all." Luna wanted to speak, to know if he was accusing *her* of something, but she held her tongue, placing her faith in the man. Not for the first time, but hopefully he wouldn't let her down this time. "Maybe she was moved by the emotion of the wedding. Though, that seems oddly out of character from the way everyone seems to have viewed her."

"When the murderer left the Princess' changing room, they apparently left an abundance of clues," he continued, by now pacing around the outside of the circle of chairs. "The Tarot card that immediately cast suspicion on Jindra Pét'a, not because of the card as such, but the revelation that she had lied by omission. The letter from a jilted lover, which, let's face it, didn't point to anyone in particular, because the Princess had, well, shall we say, experience." He paused at this, almost embarrassed by what he had said, and Luna noticed that several people in the room failed to look up, for fear of meeting someone else's eyes. "The shoeprint in the blood, which couldn't have been Prince Michael's, but at the same time couldn't have been anyone else's. A letter from Mr Reese, or Mr Regan, threatening the Princess. A red petal, which pointed to three men who couldn't possibly have been the killer, but at the same time, thanks to Madame Pét'a, we discovered anyone could have got to the Princess without being noticed. An antique hairpin that Princess Stephanie automatically claimed, despite the fact that it was most definitely not hers. A B or an R dramatically scrawled in lipstick on a mirror, pointing to...well, to half the room, really. A missing glass, a missing knife. A forest of clues. But by themselves, meaningless. After all, what motive could these people have?

"Yes, Princess Lauren was not well liked, by all accounts. She had dalliances with a number of people, including Ms Rochique, Prince Lucas and Princess Stephanie, Mr Shelby and Mr Regan. She got around, as it were. But Ms Rochique was not upset by this. She had moved on with her life. It was a dalliance in the past." Luna only realised now she had been holding her breath when this clearing of her name occurred, and she let out a sigh of relief. "Prince Lucas, however, had not. Nor had Mr Regan, but Mr Regan did not see the Princess after she came to the Hall. Mr Shelby did, as did Princess Stephanie, though for the latter there was no shame in the affair, rather she now had insight into the sort of person Princess Lauren truly was. And she wasn't the only one."

"If you know who the killer is, why not just say it?" Clayton Reese suddenly demanded, and Beauséjour smiled a little.

"The drama of it?" he asked, innocently, and Reese stood up in anger. Beauséjour held up his hands. "No, I'm...I'm not serious. Let's say that if we go through it step by step, then Inspector Kelinaw and Mr Burton will be more convinced that I haven't overlooked something. After all, I need to back up my accusation."

"Sit down, Mr Reese," Inspector Kelinaw said, and Reese looked at her in annoyance, before taking his seat again.

"Let us look at the people who visited the Princess when she arrived at the Hall and got changed into the red dress that should have stunned us all if we'd have seen it. The first person to see her was Beddows, who was instructed to bring the Princess a drink. Then her old friends, Mr and Mrs Blake. This was followed by Prince Lucas, and then Madame Pét'a. Princess Stephanie, along with Count and Countess Vladan and then Mr Barrera to check on her appreciation of the menu. We know that Princess Stephanie had motive to kill, and Countess Vladan had taken this same anger on herself. Prince Lucas also had a motive, though it was more primal." Lucas went bright red, marking yet another humiliation for someone in the room. Beauséjour wasn't going to make many friends tonight, Luna reflected. "Mr and Mrs Blake, a pair that had been blackmailed by the Princess for years because they had swindled her father out of his business, now faced the problem that the Princess no longer needed their money, and exposure was almost inevitable. Madame Pét'a of course is a fraud. Did she want to kill? Maybe, though Princess Lauren's revelations about her are hardly news. Mr Barrera seems not to have a motive, but Princess Lauren was not a person to treat the hired help well, as Ms Birman can attest to. And Mr Barrera is particularly sensitive."

"What the hell is that supposed to mean?" Barrera bellowed. Beauséjour simply held out both his hands, as if to say, *point made*. "Zakaria Barrera is the artist," Barrera sulked. "Of course I am sensitive."

"However, we are forgetting a small group of people. After the Princess took so long, Mr Shelby was sent to find her. He failed and Lord Pero attempted to get a response. He also failed; Ms Lora and Prince Michael then tried. Each of them found the door locked. Did Mr Barrera lock it on his way out? Or is one of them lying? Or, perhaps, we are overlooking Mr Solomon Burton, the chief of security. Another angry employee treated abysmally by Princess Lauren. He had the ability to lock any door here. Mr Burton's timeline is the most nebulous, as he could be anywhere at any when. Everyone says they saw him, but no one can say precisely when. Either way, the door was finally opened and Dr Kilman was brought in to examine the body." Burton opened his mouth to say something, but Beauséjour simply continued on.

"And that brings us back to the cause of death. Ms Lora claims that when they found the body it had not been stabbed, but perhaps she didn't see the blood because of the red dress? Perhaps she was so shocked she didn't look closely enough at her friend. We know that Prince Michael couldn't even approach the body, so maybe neither did Ms Lora."

"I didn't," Dione said. "I said it was too much."

"No," Beauséjour nodded, taking in her words, "it appears that Ms Rochique, Mr Regan, Ms Lora, Prince Michael and Lady Jacinta are all in the clear, as they did not encounter Princess Lauren in the Hall at any point when she was alive."

"Well, it's nice to know I'm off the hook," Luna heard Prince Michael mutter to Lord Pero.

"Yet there was something else bothering me about this case ever since we discovered the body," Beauséjour said. "Why did the murderer throw the murder weapon away? We all knew that the Princess had been stabbed, we all knew that it was a knife that had done it, and we had the gloves that the murderer was wearing, which meant…which meant that there was no concrete evidence on the murder weapon itself. There was no DNA, no fingerprints, nothing that would tie the knife to the killer, and as such, the question remained in my mind, *why throw the murder weapon away if there was nothing to be gained from this?* It could be a simple moment of panic on the part of the killer, but no…if that were the case, the gloves would be gone as well. And then I realised I was looking at this the wrong way. There was only one reason that the murder weapon was thrown away." He had managed to time his pacing so that he had ended up behind Prince Michael, and he placed his hands on the chair back as he addressed the entire room.

"Because it wasn't the murder weapon." This time the gasps of surprise were audible.

"I know what I saw," protested Dr Kilman. "I'm not an idiot," but Beauséjour either hadn't heard him or just didn't care.

"It was just another in the layer upon layer of clues that were being left around to misdirect me. We thought the knife was the murder weapon and as such we concentrated on it, when we should have been looking in another direction. And who told us the knife was the murder weapon? Doctor Kilman."

"Excuse me?" Kilman said incredulously.

"It seems scarcely credible that Doctor Kilman could have made such an obvious mistake." Beauséjour said. "But then," he added, staring at the man directly, "he had been drinking. In fact, he was known for drinking. I wonder if perhaps he had been drunk when he examined Princess Lauren the first time and his hands wandered. A secret being held over a precarious career?"

"I have something to say," Borna Vanya suddenly said, standing up.

"It would be nice, given you've said very little of use to date," Beauséjour said drily.

"It couldn't have been Fabian, because I was making love to him as soon as we got to the hall. We were interrupted when he was summoned to look at the Princess' body. I was on my knees in the middle of…"

"Yes, yes," Beauséjour interrupted her. "We get the idea. You've been looking at each other all night, giggling away. I don't think there's anyone who hadn't worked it out."

"Old people sex," Luna heard Kendal Leigh mutter. "So gross."

"It doesn't matter anyway," Beauséjour said. "The stabbing was done after Princess Lauren had already been killed. It seemed frenzied and impulsive, but perhaps there was so much stabbing because that's what the murderer wanted us to think. And so, we go back to wondering precisely how the Princess was murdered. If she wasn't stabbed, how, exactly, did she die? And when?

"Was it by poison? No. Mr Burton was telling the truth. Mr Beddows didn't ever take a drink to the Princess. Another angry employee, using the small amount of power he had to make his new mistress' life a little less bearable. And it was a little less bearable, because she needed that drink."

There were more than a few people who glanced at Beddows during this, but the butler remained tight lipped, though it was clear that he was not happy about the revelation. It explained the glass, though, Luna reflected.

"But there's also been one guest that was puzzling me," said Beauséjour. "Lady Jacinta Daniels. An interesting guest. Someone very few people here know. And by very few, I mean one. Ms Rochique thought she recognised Lady Daniels, but couldn't quite place from where. Lady Daniels isn't even on the guest list. Because her name isn't Lady Daniels, is it?" Beauséjour looked at Lady Jacinta Daniels, and while she met his gaze, Luna could immediately see that confidence had drained from her, somewhat. However, Beauséjour's comment about recognising Jacinta Daniels was curious. After all, she thought it had been from the reception. Had she given him the impression that she had recognised the woman elsewhere? *Had* she recognised the woman from elsewhere. It was true that, even after deciding she recognised Daniels from the ceremony, something had been nagging at the back of her mind. "Luna mentioned someone to me earlier, and it got me thinking. Daniels. Storm. An interesting word association," Beauséjour was saying. "What do we know about Lady Daniels? Perhaps Lady Daniels isn't Lady Daniels, but rather the Daniels comes from the word association with Storm. Perhaps Ms Rochique's memory is hazy because the last time she met Lady Daniels it was when she was living the high life with Princess Lauren and her friend Carly Robyn Storm," Beauséjour said, and Luna's mouth dropped open. He was absolutely right! That was Carly Storm. From…oh, from all those years ago. "Perhaps, in fact, Lady Daniels *is* Carly Robyn Storm, and that is why Ms Rochique vaguely remembers her? The former band mate and business partner of Princess Lauren. Former? Or perhaps co-conspirator would be more apposite." He held her gaze through the entire speech, and Daniels never broke eye contact.

"That's very good," Jacinta – Carly said. "You certainly deserve the praise that everybody has heaped on you, Professor. I didn't kill her though. So yes, I'm here under false pretences. But I'm not a murderer. And as her co-conspirator, why would I kill her? I don't get any of the money we were going to fleece off the Prince." Beauséjour smiled at her, nodding his head, apparently in agreement.

"There is something that Ms Rochique said had me thinking," he said. "She said that Princess Lauren was crying when she spoke with Lady…Ms Storm. What sort of conversation could have taken place that would make the Princess cry? This seems out of character for the Princess, especially when her gold-digging plans were coming to fruition. And then we remember something Ms Lora said. She mentioned that Princess Lauren didn't like the groomsmen's boutonniere. They weren't *her type of flower*." Beauséjour wandered over to Hunter Shelby and took the flower from his lapel, much to the groomsman's surprise.

"But why?" Beauséjour mused aloud. "Perhaps because she was allergic to them. Though who's allergic to chrysanthemums? A few people, possibly." He studied the flower, turning it over in his hands. "Though double chrysanthemums do look a lot like dahlias. And allergies to those are much more common." He handed the flower back to Shelby. "And like that, it becomes clear. Princess Lauren wasn't crying because of Ms Storm, she was crying from allergies. The red flower in the bouquet was a dahlia, not a double chrysanthemum. An easy mistake to make. And the Princess was allergic to them. Fatally allergic. She wasn't worried though. Why would she? Those closest to her knew the flower she was allergic to." He turned to address the entire room again.

"Each of you who spoke to the Princess when you met her in the reception hall thought she had been rude, by ignoring you, or simply not paying attention. But the fact of the matter is, Mr Beddows was probably the last person to see her alive. By the time Mr and Mrs Blake had their argument, which was little more than two people shouting at a third, she was already dead." Around the room, everyone looked astonished. Luna could see that those who had met the princess were clearly going through the previous conversations in their head, and each of them, one by one, came to the same conclusion. Princess Lauren hadn't replied to any of them at any point. Axton Beauséjour was right.

"So, who put the flower in the bouquet?" he posed. "Remember, according to Countess Vladan, it was an all-white wedding and yet, Mrs Blake said that she thought the red flower in the bouquet was tacky. She noticed this because she saw the bouquet when Ms Birman took it away from the changing room. Ms Birman said that the Princess was going to change into a red dress, hinted at by the red flower in the bouquet. So, it seems someone put the flower into the bouquet *after* the ceremony. It was a white bouquet when I spoke to her, so it wasn't me, or either of the bridesmaids. And the others who saw Ms Rochique, Mr Regan and Ms Storm never mentioned them carrying a red flower." He paused, letting the scenario sink in. "No, only Princess Lauren herself could have tampered with the bouquet."

"You can't be serious!" Carly Storm said, shocked by the implication.

"That's insane," Kendal Leigh added. Luna looked around the room and saw that nearly everyone seemed to be outraged. Despite the woman being someone they all hated, the very idea she had committed her own murder seemed an anathema to them.

Well, not quite everyone. Prince Michael seemed to be in some sort of reverie, and Beddows and Birman were also standing quietly at the back, their faces unchanged. Luna glanced at Beauséjour who seemed to be drinking in their responses.

"Only Princess Lauren," Beauséjour repeated. But then, he turned. "And her loyal maid."

All eyes turned to Amy Birman, who visibly flinched under the scrutiny. Beauséjour's eyes drilled into her, and for a moment she turned away, but it was Beddows who blocked her path. She looked around the room, as though searching for something, but then turned to Beauséjour.

"I didn't," she protested weakly, but the guilt was written across her face.

"Oh, you definitely did, Amy," Beauséjour said softly. Amy did not look Beauséjour in the face. Instead, she lowered her head, not looking at anyone. Beddows seemed torn, uncertain whether to leap to her defence, or to condemn.

Luna watched Inspector Kelinaw step forward, and Burton raised his hands somewhat resigned. Kelinaw crossed to the main door and opened it, and seemingly before she had time to say or do anything, two police had materialised.

"You're under arrest Ms Birman," Kelinaw intoned. "For the murder of Princess Lauren."

Amy looked to Prince Michael, but he was unable to meet her gaze. She opened her mouth to say something, but then turned and accepted her fate.

Chapter Two

Just One More Thing

Luna had to admit she was slightly surprised by the first words out of Prince Michael's mouth. "Well done, Professor. I had hoped you would be efficient, but I didn't think..." He ended his sentence, waving his hands slightly. Perhaps he didn't know what he thought; Luna could imagine it must be enormously difficult for him. Regardless of how he felt, he was unable to express it, and Luna felt a huge swell of sympathy for him.

And yet, Luna thought, Beauséjour seemed not to. He was behaving in a way that was very unexpected. He didn't respond, didn't say anything. Merely sunk into a chair, not acknowledging the Prince, not listening to what was said.

"I think we can let the guests go now," Prince Michael said, nodding to Burton, and accordingly, the security man turned and indicated the door. Luna wasn't quite sure what the time was, but given everything, guessed it had to be very early in the morning.

The departure of the guests was like something from a horror movie; a gaggle of people, zombie like and equally pale faced, shuffling towards the door, no expression on their faces. Some, like Clayton Reese, paused momentarily as they passed Axton Beauséjour, as though they wanted to get into a fight with the man, and hold him personally responsible for everything that had happened. But the moment passed, and they seemed to lose the desire, or at the very least questioned "what's the point?" Or maybe they realised that the past had finally caught up with them, and it was time to pay the piper. Luna wondered what would happen to the Reeses. Would they get away with their manipulation of Lauren's father's company, or would they turn themselves in. If Beauséjour suggested an audit of the company, a lot of things would come out (if they hadn't already).

The others were less resistant. When they passed Beauséjour there was a look of...apology? It was hard to say. Killman, Jindra, Regan...it was as though they had brought hell down on themselves and wanted to let the messenger know they were sorry for the way things had proceeded. But like the anger of the others, it came to nothing. The wind had been taken from their sails, and there was nothing anyone could do about it. Yes, the future was very uncertain for a lot of people.

Finally, as Inspector Kelinaw returned to let them know that everyone had left, there was only Prince Michael, Princess Stephanie, Luna, Burton and Beddows left in the room with Beauséjour, Luna and Kelinaw.

"Time to leave," Michael said, a little apologetically.

"I wonder," Beauséjour said, so softly Luna had to strain to hear what he said. "Why you invited me to this wedding. I thought it might have been genuinely out of respect. But I wonder if it was simply to prove that you were cleverer than your old lecturer?"

Luna had once appeared on stage to a crowd that definitely did not like her. As the silence descended on the room, Luna honestly felt that the silence the crowd had given her that night was less awkward than what was happening now.

"I beg your pardon?" Michael said.

"I was your guest," Beauséjour said. "Seated at your table."

"Of course you were," Michael replied, confused.

"So why was I sitting beside Luna?" The silence returned, but this time the awkwardness was clearly coming from just one direction.

Luna could have kicked herself as she realised the point Beauséjour was making. She was surely at the wrong table. And yet, she couldn't quite see why this was so significant.

"You thought it would unsettle me. Put me off. Seating me beside someone from my past; a mistake I'd made coming back to haunt me. You wound me up and set me off like a kid's toy, but just to make sure I didn't find the truth, the whole truth and nothing but the truth, you put a little obstacle in the way, hoping that I'd lose confidence. That I'd fail."

"Why would I do that?" Michael asked, but Luna could hear the hesitation in his voice.

"We've spent a lot of time talking about Princess Lauren's dalliances," Beauséjour said. "But we know that Ms Lora was very keen on you, but we don't know if there was ever a proper relationship there. Lord Pero said you'd had an affair, but again, we all thought that was Dione and was nothing more than a potential rather than a concrete probability. So, when Mr Burton overheard you saying to someone that they would be together soon, that someone was perhaps not Ms Lora. Perhaps there's a reason Mr Beddows never lets Ms Birman speak. Perhaps he knows things that he doesn't want to reveal out of loyalty to his master." Luna's eyebrows rose as she realised what Professor Axton Beauséjour was saying; the truth of his words. Beauséjour finally turned in his chair and looked Prince Michael directly in the eye. As he continued to speak, each word spelled out a truth.

"What exactly are you trying to say?" Prince Michael said, for the first time in the night his voice tinged with danger.

"After Mr Barrera left, there was talk about how long the Princess was taking. Ms Birman probably overheard this, so she slipped down the corridor, unguarded by the very slack Mr Burton, and locked the door, preventing anyone from getting in. Before this, however, she set about leaving the clues that would confuse everyone. Soon, Mr Shelby and Lord Pero were unable to enter. Then Prince Michael and Ms Lora got Mr Burton to open the door. They walked in, the saw the dead body, but Dione Lora didn't lie - there was no blood; Princess Lauren hadn't been stabbed at that point. When Ms Lora went to get Dr Kilman, you had to act fast. You donned your gloves, took the steak knife you had brought with you, and repeatedly stabbed the Princess. Then you pocketed the knife. When Dr Kilman arrived, you approached the body and made the footprint, adding another clue that worked in your favour. Kilman pronounced her dead, but didn't really spend too much time examining the body. As drunk as he was, even he could see the stab wounds. The police were summoned, everyone was locked away. But you weren't concerned. After all, you're a prince. Who's going to search you? There was plenty of time for you to hide the knife." By now Beauséjour stood in front of the Prince Michael, who looked at him with a cold, amused regard.

"Saying things doesn't make it real, Professor," Prince Michael said. "You don't have any evidence for either Kelinaw or Burton to act on. It's just a speculative tale, in the desperate hope that a confession might come. But as I didn't do it, I won't be confessing."

"It's not speculative, your highness," Beauséjour said. "And we both know there is proof."

"What proof is that?" Now Prince Michael smiled, clearly confident in having set up Beauséjour. The law professor looked around, and raised his eyebrows, having apparently got what he wanted. He strolled over to Beddows.

"Could I borrow that please?" He handed his cane to the butler in exchange for something and limped back to the Prince. As he did, he pulled on a white glove, clearly having obtained it from the waiter. "You don't mind, do you?" Beauséjour said, and before Prince Michael could say anything, Beauséjour leaned forward and pulled the Prince's jacket open, reaching in with his gloved hand. The Prince was wrong-footed, so surprised at this personal invasion he failed to react, and so Beauséjour stepped back, the gloved hand holding a steak knife, clearly coated in dry blood. Now it was Beauséjour who had an amused look on his face. "That, your highness, is not speculation."

"How dare you," thundered the Prince, finally getting his voice. "How dare you touch…" But he was cut off from his rant as, to his shock, a hand was placed firmly on his shoulder.

"Your highness," Solomon Burton muttered.

"Get your hands off me, Burton."

"Don't make me use force, your highness," Burton continued. Inspector Kelinaw had joined Beauséjour, collecting the knife in a plastic evidence bag. The Prince was beyond furious, and yet as he looked around, the faces of everyone looked back with a mixture of horror and disgust. "You hypocrites," spat Michael. "None of you liked her."

"That doesn't mean we wanted her dead," Stephanie said, and she spoke for everyone.

"Come along, your highness," Burton said.

"It will be alright," the Prince said, seemingly to himself. "I'll protect Amy. They seem to forget about a King's pardon." He looked around triumphantly, but his sister's face held nothing but contempt.

"You're not the King," Princess Stephanie said. "And you never will be."

Chapter Three

A Quiet Ending

The Royal Arms, Reidon

"You're impressed," Inspector Kelinaw said, and Luna gave her a look.

"I never said I didn't think he was good," she said, hearing the sulk in her own voice. "He just seems to enjoy the sound of his own voice too much. And he doesn't always give a lot of thought to the people around him when he's determined to get to the killer. He's like a hurricane. Great for the environment but not really all that good for the inhabitants." She had gone down the corridor to see that the police had moved in completely now, cleaning up and collecting all the evidence. Statements were being taken before the guests were officially released to go home, though the Royal family had already departed, with Prince Michael being taken away to have a serious discussion with Inspector Kelinaw. Although given the Inspector was still at the barracks, she assumed that the discussion was a little way off.

"How often does he actually solve murders?" Kelinaw asked, a little incredulously.

"More often than you think, surprisingly," Luna sighed.

"I'm surprised you'd know given how much travelling you do," came a voice from behind her, and Luna turned to see Beauséjour coming towards her, leaning on his cane more than she had seen him do for some time.

"Sometimes I make the effort to see what you're up to," Luna said, and she found herself smiling despite herself.

"Well, I need to go and do some processing," Kelinaw said. "There're still things that need to be sorted out."

"Before Prince Michael goes to jail?" Luna asked, and Beauséjour let out a sigh, which Luna initially didn't quite understand. "What?" she asked.

"He's not going to jail," Kelinaw said, a little sadly.

"What do you mean? He confessed. We all heard it. The Professor found the murder weapon on him," protested Luna.

"He's the heir apparent," Beauséjour reminded her. "He's not going to jail. Oh, Princess Stephanie will ensure he never takes the throne, but like all Royals who find themselves in scandals, they simply slip away, to be wheeled out at the odd funeral or wedding, but they never face the consequences of their actions." Luna suddenly felt very sad.

"So, Lauren will never see justice?" Beauséjour and Kelinaw both knew that the question was rhetorical, and so they simply lowered their heads, feeling much the same as Luna did. "And people say the music industry is corrupt," she muttered. Inspector Kelinaw looked awkward, before finally saying goodbye.

"Thank you for your help, Professor Beauséjour," the detective said. "It certainly made my job a lot easier. And meant I didn't have to spend time fighting Solomon Burton. It was an honour to meet you Ms Rochique. I never mentioned that my daughter was a fan. I may have to listen to more of your music."

"You should bring her to a concert," grinned Luna.

"You should have one in Crovania," the Inspector replied, and with that she turned and headed off.

"Where to now, Ms Rochique?" Beauséjour wondered.

"Oh, I have to go back to LA to do some recording, and then I'm home for a bit before I go on tour later this year. This wedding fell at just the right time to get out to do something."

"What a life you lead," Beauséjour smiled, indulgently.

"What about you?"

"Oh, I'll just head back to university and continue to lecture, such is my life. I imagine my mother and my cat will have missed me," Beauséjour said, the smile never leaving his face.

"You don't care that Prince Michael isn't going to jail, do you? You're just happy you solved the mystery," Luna suddenly accused, and Beauséjour had the decency to look hurt.

"That's not fair. At the end of the day, I'd like to think I wanted justice," he paused as he looked out the window to see the guests departing. "I suppose the truth is the moment I realised it was Prince Michael, I knew there would be no impact. I suppose I had more time to get used to the fact that it was going to be an empty outcome. Lauren Foster won't get the justice she deserved."

"It's just not fair," Luna muttered.

"No," agreed Beauséjour, and to her surprise, he reached out and clasped her shoulder. "We can't control other people, Luna. You know that. All we can do is the right thing. If the world can't support us in that, that's not on us. When we meet up after all this," and for a moment Luna wondered exactly what he meant, "Lauren will know what you did for her."

"No one will care when we're all dead," Luna said pointedly.

"That's very true," Beauséjour agreed, but Luna wasn't quite sure they were on the same page. He stuck out his hand, and she took it. "It was honestly lovely to see you again, Luna. I'm very glad I did."

And as he walked away, Luna realised that she was as well.

When Lauren Met Axton

The Church of The Divine Manifestation, Reidon

Five hours ago

Lauren Foster glanced into the crowd and was relieved to see that Carly's face was looking back at her. She saw the small wink, and felt herself get stronger and more confident. Plans were coming to fruition and soon she and Carly would be living the life of luxury that they had always planned. That they *deserved*. Because why not? It wasn't like Michael cared. She was fairly certain that he was banging the maid. Not that she didn't understand why, she was a cute little thing and was definitely worth a second look. But if she had any guilt about conning the Prince, it evaporated every time she saw him coming in hot and sweaty after "sorting out some details" with the maid.

Plus, that toffee nosed butler definitely knew what was going on and he didn't have her back. He was a piece of work. None of the staff particularly liked her. None of them made the effort to get to know her or embrace her. They were all so wrapped up in their own little world, the idea of accepting a stranger into it was completely beyond them.

It built up resentment. And it meant that doing little things, like teasing Lucas that there might be a chance she'd sleep with him, or getting drunk and actually sleeping with Stephanie, didn't generate any guilt whatsoever. Part of her even felt a certain satisfaction knowing that she could almost call bingo on the royal family.

As she glanced into the crowd, she also saw Luna Rochique, her blue hair making her stand out from the rest of the crowd. She was standing next to Dana Spectra. How amazing to think that an average nobody from Scullin, like herself, was getting married, and was able to invite superstars to her wedding.

It made her feel important. No, more than that. It was proof that she had made it. She was *somebody*. All the people who laughed at her and put her down were laughing on the other side of their stupid faces now. She had proven beyond a shadow of a doubt that she was cared about. Rockstars and supermodels came when she clicked. She was the definition of an It girl. Her mother was probably reading about her in some crappy woman's magazine.

In fact, she thought she might even pay her mother a visit and see what it was like still living in a slum and looking at the daughter she had said would never make it. She was so close to being the actual queen of a foreign country. Never make it, indeed.

Cameron Regan was sitting in the crowd as well, looking moody and dark. God, he was still so sexy. There probably wasn't any reason not to get him back in bed as soon as the chance came along, really. There was, Lauren reflected, no end to the things she could do. With Michael being busy doing king-stuff, she had the opportunity to do pretty much anything she liked. Or anyone she liked.

She would move Carly in as soon as possible, that was the first thing. And then they would set out to make the castle their own. She couldn't help but smile at the thought.

The possibilities were endless from this point on. This was actually the first day of the rest of her life.

Turning away, she was ushered down the corridor by security guards, Dione and Kendal in tow, with Amy bringing up the rear as they headed for the room where she would compose herself before taking the car to the reception. She had handed her bouquet to Amy because she was absolutely tired of carrying that around, and quite frankly she wanted to get out of her dress, but unfortunately, she couldn't do that until they reached the…what was the place? Some old, dank barracks or another. Honestly, she needed the whole day to be over with. Thank god they had the official photographs and portraits done the day before.

"We'll just go to the car and see if it's ready?" Dione asked and Lauren gave a nod, rather than answering. She wasn't really in the mood to talk anymore. What she really wanted was a drink. As she sat down, she saw a red flower on the table, and irritably, she stuck it in the middle of her bouquet, much to Amy's surprise. Also, rather surprisingly, she sneezed.

"Are you alright, ma'am?" Amy asked. Lauren glared at her.

"Go and make sure I can…*ahchoo!* God!" Frustrated, Lauren sneezed two more times and looked around for a tissue. Amy dithered, and Lauren glared at her, and the maid hurried out.

As she did, Lauren was a little surprised to see a man standing at the door, holding a distinctive cane, and wearing a beret and a scarf. Now she thought about it, she remembered seeing him in the church as well.

"Sorry," she said, and was a little surprised when he held out a tissue, which she took gratefully. "Do I know you?"

"Axton Beauséjour," he said, and offered his hand with a smile. "Your husband invited me to the wedding. I thought I should do the right thing and introduce myself. I doubt we'll have much chance to chat at the reception."

"Oh, no, probably not," Lauren agreed. "I have to get changed, there'll be dinner and dancing. It'll be quite the affair I assume. Does Michael know you well?"

"I used to lecture him in law," Beauséjour replied.

"Oh," Lauren said. "He has mentioned you a few times. You made quite the impression on him. I met him after he had finished classes with you, but he did talk about your passion for the law."

"Well, that is true," grinned Beauséjour. "The law isn't perfect, but it's the best form of justice we have." He reached inside his jacket, and produced a clear tube, which he handed over to Lauren. Inside was a white rose made of what was possibly glass, with a singular butterfly on one of the petals, its wings, shades of scarlet and violet. The rose was lit from the inside, making the butterfly sparkle. "I wanted to get you something, but as I don't know you, I hope this will do."

"Oh, it's beautiful," Lauren breathed, and she was surprised that she actually meant it. "I love roses. Chrysanthemums aren't really my kind of flower, if I'm honest, but I love a rose. Thank you Mr Beauséjour."

"Professor," he corrected, and she looked at him sharply, but the beauty of the flower hit her and she was spell bound again.

"I hope," Beauséjour said, "that it will light your way, for better or for worse, for richer or for poorer, in sickness and in health. It will glow brighter the more you love and the more you cherish. I hope you like it."

And without hesitation, mesmerised by the beautiful gift, Lauren muttered:

"I do."

Also by Rachele Alson

It's easy to be popular in high school if you're prepared to fit in. But when you get to university, sometimes you need a better way to be number one. Essie was one of the most popular girls in secondary school. When she turns up dead a few weeks into tertiary it seems the popularity got to her. But Lavender and Celestine Strange aren't so sure. To them the death seems a little too convenient. And when the people around Essie turnout to have dark secrets, their suspicions grow. The Strange sisters are convinced that Essie was murdered. They just need to find out who the killer is before they strike again.